"Of course we can solve mysteries as well as grown-up detectives." This was Nancy Drew's answer to a question from a group gathered in her living room in River Heights. "How would you like to form a detective club and have meetings at my house? Later we can solve some mysteries. What do you say?"

Cheers and applause greeted this remark. Nancy suggests that you readers work along with the club and learn how to become amateur detectives.

*"One! Two! Three! Go!"*

# THE
# NANCY DREW
# SLEUTH BOOK

## CLUES to GOOD SLEUTHING
### by Carolyn Keene

Grosset & Dunlap

GROSSET & DUNLAP
Published by the Penguin Group
Penguin Group (USA) Inc., 375 Hudson Street,
New York, New York 10014, U.S.A.
Penguin Group (Canada), 90 Eglinton Avenue East, Suite 700, Toronto, Ontario,
Canada M4P 2Y3
(a division of Pearson Penguin Canada Inc.)
Penguin Books Ltd, 80 Strand, London WC2R 0RL, England
Penguin Ireland, 25 St Stephen's Green, Dublin 2, Ireland
(a division of Penguin Books Ltd)
Penguin Group (Australia), 250 Camberwell Road, Camberwell, Victoria 3124, Australia
(a division of Pearson Australia Group Pty Ltd)
Penguin Books India Pvt Ltd, 11 Community Centre,
Panchsheel Park, New Delhi–110 017, India
Penguin Group (NZ), 67 Apollo Drive, Mairangi Bay,
Auckland 1311, New Zealand (a division of Pearson New Zealand Ltd)
Penguin Books (South Africa) (Pty) Ltd, 24 Sturdee Avenue,
Rosebank, Johannesburg 2196, South Africa

Penguin Books Ltd, Registered Offices:
80 Strand, London WC2R 0RL, England

The Library of Congress has cataloged the original edition as follows:
Library of Congress Control Number: 78058209

ISBN 978-0-448-44568-7     10 9 8 7 6 5 4 3 2 1

# CONTENTS

# CHAPTER I

# THE BURGLAR'S NOTE
## *Handwriting Clues*

"WHO brought a mystery today?" Nancy Drew asked the six girls in her Detective Club. This was the first meeting of the newly formed group, and the subject was to be handwriting.

"I have a good mystery," Cathy Chase, Nancy's blond, blue-eyed friend who loved to wear light blue sweaters, replied. "My mother always leaves house money in a coffee can in a kitchen cupboard. It's used by everyone in the family, and little notes are left about how much is taken out by whom. This morning Mother discovered that all the money was gone, and so were our notes."

"I'll bet someone in the Chase family is playing a joke," Sue Fletcher called out. She was a brunette with short, curly hair and black eyes.

"No," Cathy replied. "The burglars left three new notes. They were written in strange handwritings."

The club members looked at one another, then at Nancy Drew. The young strawberry blond detective smiled. "The notes could have been left by one, two, or three burglars." She asked Cathy, "Did you bring the messages?"

"Yes." Cathy took three slips of paper from her handbag. She handed them to Nancy, who held them up for the other girls to see. Each note was in a different script. The first one said: *Thank you.* The next one said: *I need this money more than you do.* The third was in an exaggerated, artificial scrawl, slanting downward at the end of the line and read: *Ha! Ha! I dare you to find me!*

Nancy stared at the notes thoughtfully. "Cathy, are you suspicious of anyone?"

"No."

"Do you think one person could have written all three notes?" Sue asked.

Nancy studied the messages closely. "There are people who can imitate other handwritings so well that even the experts cannot be sure, but it's rare. Let's see if we can find similarities in the shape of the letters, their slant, pressure, spacing, and size."

"What difference does letter size make?" Karen Carpenter wanted to know. She was full of fun.

"Letter size makes a lot of difference," Nancy answered. "A person who enjoys activity and achievement tends to have a large handwriting. He or she takes on a large task with excitement, where others often feel

"Ha! Ha! I dare you to find me!" the note read.

intimidated. It is someone who is always on the go, who's enthusiastic and interested in large issues, usually bored by details, and often restless and impatient."

"Like you," Cathy said to Karen.

"That's true," Karen reflected. "I do make my letters rather large. What about people who write small letters?"

"People who write small are usually thorough and think things through. They're able to face life without getting upset and are often observant. Sometimes they like to be aloof from others, but actually they are often more interested in other people than those with large handwriting." Nancy paused.

"I have an uncle who squeezes so much onto a page, you can hardly read it," Karen said.

Nancy nodded. "It suggests that he's stingy."

"That he is," said Karen.

The girls scrutinized the messages for a few minutes, then came to the conclusion that they were most likely written by different people.

"Can you tell a man's writing from a woman's?" asked Peg Goodale, who had brown hair and large brown eyes.

"Not always," Nancy replied. "But you can make an educated guess whether or not the script looks masculine or feminine. I think that these notes look like they were written by men. They were written with heavy pressure and the crosses of certain letters like *t* and *f* are very long—two indicators of a masculine hand. What does everyone think?"

The girls agreed with Nancy. Nancy took the first message and laid it on the table for everyone to see. "Let's start with this one and find out what it tells us about the writer. The letters are spaced pretty far apart and are slanted to the right."

"What does that mean?" Karen asked.

"A forward slant indicates more heart than head control, an outgoing person who enjoys being with others. The wide spacing shows that he likes plenty of room, is spontaneous, and is probably a generous person."

"He doesn't sound like a wily old burglar," remarked Honey Rushmore, the secretary. She had honey-colored hair, rosy cheeks, and gray eyes.

"No, he doesn't," Nancy agreed. "Especially since his writing is also clear and legible, which means he doesn't try to hide anything. His pressure is light, which makes him a gentle and sensitive person."

"Shall we rule him out as a suspect?" Sue asked.

"Yes," Nancy replied. "Let's check the next one." The girls scanned the second note closely.

"This man is more controlled by intellect than emotion," Nancy said, "because he makes his letters straight. He's also more reserved and self-reliant. His pressure is medium, which suggests that he is healthy, and fond of people and things. You see, heavy pressure indicates intensity, while a mixture of light, medium, and heavy often shows a physical or mental disturbance."

"His spaces are narrow but even," Sue pointed out.

"The evenness means he's in control of every situation," said Nancy. "And look at the *e* at the end of *more*. It has an extended, ascending final stroke. That makes him a warm person. Also, his *o* is open, meaning he's honest. When *o*'s and *a*'s are closed and knotted, the writer is highly secretive and reserved, often insincere. But not this writer."

"Well, I'd say that eliminates number two from our list of suspects," Sue declared. "What about the last note?"

The message, *Ha! Ha! I dare you to find me!* was examined by each girl. The words, sprawled downward in a slightly zigzagging angle, fascinated them.

"This script doesn't appeal to me," Karen decided.

Nancy's eyes twinkled. "He's writing with a backward slant. That indicates he's inhibited and more interested in things than people. He doesn't make friends easily and could be suspicious and cold. His exaggerated, artificial style suggests dishonesty. Also, the fact that the letters vary in size and pressure is uneven makes me think that he's unstable."

"I notice that many letters are pointed," Karen said. "Does that have any significance?"

"Yes. In combination with the backward slant, it could mean the man is cruel."

"What if he's left-handed?" Cathy asked. "Does the rule about the backward slant still stand?"

"No. Left-handed people often can't control their writing from slanting backward."

"I doubt this fellow is left-handed," Karen said. "Just look at this note. I think he's every bit as mean as his script looks."

"I see something else," Sue spoke up. "The *I* is much taller than his other caps."

"He's vain," Nancy said. "That could explain—" She was thoughtful for a moment, until Sue urged, "Explain what?"

"Why he bothered with these notes. He could have taken the money without leaving any clues. But if he's conceited and vain, he might just do a thing like this, thinking he's smart."

Karen laughed. "He certainly appears to be a totally despicable character. Cathy, do you know anyone who fits this description?"

Cathy shook her head. "Maybe my mother does. I'll call her." She went to the phone and reported their findings about the handwriting. "Do you know anyone who matches this description?" she asked.

"Man or woman?" Mrs. Chase inquired.

"Probably a man."

There was a long pause, then Mrs. Chase said, "No, not really. Why don't you all come over here and look around? Perhaps the thief left other clues."

Cathy covered the receiver with her hand and repeated her mother's suggestion to the other girls.

"Great idea!" Nancy called out. "Let's go!"

When the club members arrived at the Chase house, they began to search the backyard. Behind a hedge, Nancy and Karen saw something suspicious. Karen picked it up.

"It's a little notebook!" she said. "It looks clean and new!"

"That means it hasn't been here long," Nancy said as the others crowded around. "What's inside?"

Karen opened the notebook.

"Various names and numbers—" Nancy began.

"The handwriting matches the third note!" Karen interrupted excitedly. "Not quite so exaggerated, but I'm sure it's the same!"

"It does!" chorused the others.

"This notebook doesn't make much sense," Nancy said. "The only notation on the first page is *Brothers, after three P.M.*"

She flipped the page. "Here are two names, *Tomlinson and Ernest.*"

"How about the next page?" Sue urged.

"Nothing but *eighty.*"

"Wasn't eighty dollars the amount left in the coffee can, Mother?" Cathy asked.

"That's right. I wonder if this is what the note refers to."

Nancy flipped through the rest of the notebook. "Nothing else," she said. Then she turned to Mrs. Chase. "Who could have seen you put money into the coffee can besides the members of your family?"

"No one," Cathy's mother replied. "Unless—unless somebody was looking in through the window."

"Who came to the door yesterday?" Nancy asked.

"Let's see. The man who cuts the grass. The trashman, who took some things from the cellar. And a deliveryman from the ice-cream store."

"What are they like?" Nancy wanted to know.

"Well, the ice-cream fellow never speaks and never smiles," Mrs. Chase replied. "Once I had to scold him for kicking our dog, who wasn't bothering him."

The members of the detective club looked at one another. Not talkative, not friendly, cruel—just like the suspect!

"Mrs. Chase," said Nancy, "do you have a signature sample or any of the deliveryman's writing?"

"I think so." Cathy's mother opened a drawer in one of the kitchen cabinets containing bills. One was a receipt for an ice-cream cake, marked *Delivered P.M.*

"That's the same handwriting!" Cathy exclaimed. "He's the thief! But how did he get into the house unnoticed?"

Nancy went to the back door. "Here's your answer. He unlocked the bolt when he delivered the ice cream. After the family was asleep, he returned, let himself in, took the money, and put the bolt back into place before leaving."

Cathy asked, "Now what do we do?"

"I'll call the police," her mother replied, "and turn your findings over to them."

She did so and was told that many people had reported a clever thief, but Nancy's deductions were the first real clues. An officer would be sent to the house at once.

When Detective Hafner heard their story, he said this was the only time the burglar had left notes.

"The thief slipped the bolt when he delivered the ice cream," Nancy explained.

"That was his undoing," Hafner declared.

Karen asked, "But where did he get the other two notes?"

The detective looked at Nancy. "What's your guess?"

"That he used some kind of excuse, or perhaps money, to get two people to write them. Detective Hafner, may I see the notebook again?"

He handed it over, and Nancy studied the strange entry. Suddenly her eyes lit up. "P.M. must be his initials! In the notation 'Brothers, after three P.M.' I thought he referred to the afternoon. But now I'm inclined to believe that P.M. had to make a delivery to someone named Brothers, after three!"

"Of course!" Detective Hafner said admiringly. "That's why the receipt for the cake was signed P.M. Now all we have to do is contact the ice-cream store and find out who P.M. is. Ladies, thanks a lot for your great work!"

The following day he phoned Nancy to say that the deliveryman had been questioned and confessed to many burglaries, including the one in Cathy Chase's home. His name was Paul Milkin.

Nancy called the members of the Detective Club to tell them the news. She also reminded them of their next meeting. "Tuesday, same place, same time," she said. "And be sure to bring a mystery!"

When Mrs. Chase heard the news, she laughed and said, "If you ladies keep this up, we won't even need a police department in this town!"

Here are some additional clues to a person's character that can be drawn from the formation of individual letters:

## CAPITALS:

A   printed—simplicity, artistic

ℒ   old-fashioned caps—respect for tradition

ℳ   high first stroke on *M*—strong wish for approval

𝒜   wide-base caps—gullible

𝒪   narrow-base caps—cautious

𝒳   ornate caps—vain

𝒟   open-top *D* or *O*—frank, generous, often talkative, gossipy

I   resourceful, severe

|   strong ego, plain tastes
    inflated loop—demands attention, warmth
    small loop simple—cautious, modest

Clue: If the *I* is bigger than other words—conceit. If the tall loop is simple—pride in work, loyalty.

## SMALL LETTERS:

𝓈   creative mind

𝓺   mathematical

𝓈   devoted to others, warmhearted

𝒹   given to silence, cautious

𝒹   tall stem—possessing great dignity, trustworthy

𝓛 open *b*—easily fooled

𝓪 𝓵 all letters with unnecessary first strokes—conventional

𝓵 𝓵 the wider the loop, the more receptive to flattery

𝓰 𝔂 return stroke extending left—immature

𝓬 refined tastes

𝓮 sharp perceptive mind, quick thinker and talker

𝓼𝓬𝓽 any small letter that is printed—creative ability, versatile, independent

### THE LETTER *T*:

𝓽 well-balanced, controlled, disciplined

𝓽 right-flying *t*—lively, quick-tempered

𝔃 indecisive

𝔃 t-bar high to left—weak, head in clouds

𝓯 star-crossed—obstinate

𝔂 looped t-bar—less sensitive and confident

𝓣 tenacious

𝔁 domineering

𝓽 initiative t—imaginative, quickly adjusts

𝓽 low t-bar—kindly, guilty, depressed

𝓵 t-bar eliminated—careless, lacking in initiative

Clue: The way the t-bar is balanced on the vertical stroke indicates a person's willpower, spirit, and drive. The t-bar is an indicator of how well someone reaches their goals.

## ENDINGS OF WORDS *E*:

*2* final absent—secretive

*ω* extended ascending final—warm

*ω* upturned hook final—humorous, very persistent, optimistic

*⌐* downturned hook final—stubborn

*•—* straight, heavy final—bitter, ill-tempered, wary

*ω* high, upcurved final—friendly

*λ* blunt downstroke final—bossy, self-assertive

*ω* selfish

*⅋* vain

*∂* sensitive

*ω* cruel

*ω* visionary

*ι* meek

*ω* emotionally disturbed

*ω* imaginative

*ℓ* shy

*ℓ* domineering

*ℓ* discreet

## ACTIVITY

Nancy suggests that you get samples of handwriting from your friends and relatives. Try to see how their various character traits match up to what you have learned.

# CHAPTER II

# THE STRANGE THUMBPRINT
## *Clues in Fingerprints*

THE front doorbell of the Drew house rang long and loudly. Nancy hurried to answer it.

Peg Goodale, a member of the young sleuth's Detective Club, rushed into the hall.

"Oh, Nancy, I have a marvelous mystery for us to solve!" she exclaimed.

"Good! But don't tell it until the rest of the girls arrive."

They did not have to wait long. Within minutes the others hurried in. With them were Bess Marvin, a slightly plump, pretty blonde, and dark-haired George Fayne, her tomboy cousin, two of Nancy's closest friends. They often helped when she was working on a case.

After the minutes of the previous meeting had been read by Honey Rushmore, the secretary, Peg was invited to speak.

"As you know," she began, "two weeks ago my grand-father died. There was no will in his safe-deposit box, but one was found in the top drawer of his library desk. Evidently, he wrote it himself. It was witnessed by a friend, now dead. On the will is a dark thumbprint."

"Your grandfather's?" Honey asked.

"No. From prints on file at police headquarters, it's obvious that the print belongs neither to Grandpa nor to his butler. Because of this fact, the executor doesn't want to accept the will as authentic."

"Why?" Sue Fletcher asked.

"Because the will may have been tampered with, or even forged."

Nancy asked if there was any question about the contents of the will.

"Yes, there is. Grandpa Goodale was wealthy and had told my parents he was leaving most of his estate to them. But in his will, only a small amount goes to them. The rest goes to a couple named Murphy, who worked for Grandpa many years ago."

Bess Marvin spoke up. "Maybe your grandfather felt sorry for them and wanted them to be comfortable in their old age."

Peg shook her head. "Grandpa was angry with them. They left him suddenly, right after my grandmother died. He was handicapped, and it was difficult for him to get around. But he insisted on staying in his own house."

"That certainly was a mean thing for the Murphys to do," George remarked. "Where are these people now?"

"We're not sure," Peg replied. "Nancy, what do you think we should do?"

"Track down whose thumbprint appears on the will."

"How?" Sue asked.

"First we'll try to find a matching print. There are no two people in the whole world with the same fingerprints, so the thumbprints are our first clue. There are many areas to which fingerprints will adhere. Hard surfaces that are nonporous show them up best. On a surface that absorbs the perspiration or oil from the skin—like unglazed paper, rough cardboard, and unfinished wood—you can't really see them. Those prints are called latent, or hidden, prints. They must be developed by using a chemical. The visible prints are usually dusted to make them show up clearly."

"But you can't take them with you as evidence, can you?" Karen asked.

"Oh yes you can. They can be photographed, or lifted by means of a rubbery tape to which the powder will stick."

"Powder?" Cathy asked.

"Right," Nancy replied. "On light surfaces you dust with lampblack, graphite, or acacia powder. On dark surfaces you use white lead or talc. Sometimes, of course, you don't need anything, because the finger that made the print had a sticky or filmy substance on it, like paint, ink, blood, or just plain dirt. They are clearly visible without having to be dusted." The young sleuth said she had been planning to discuss fingerprints during one of their club meetings. "For that reason I bought some putty for us to practice on."

Nancy opened a bag and took out a small chunk for each girl, together with a paper towel. They flattened the pieces, then George called out, "One! Two! Three! Go!"

Giggling, the members of the Detective Club pushed one finger after another onto the putty until they had prints of all ten fingers.

Bess grinned as she stared at hers. "The circle in the middle of my third finger looks like a lopsided pear."

"Only you would say that," her cousin said.

*"Hmph!"* Bess replied while George glanced at her prints.

"I see an apple on the index finger, a banana on your pinky, and a chocolate custard pie on your thumb!" George teased her cousin.

After they had compared notes and joked about the differences in their arches, loops, and whorls of which a fingerprint consists, Nancy said, "Now I think we'd better get back to the mystery of Grandfather Goodale's will with the thumbprint on it. By the way, Peg, where did you say the print is?"

"On the back of the last page. There are three pages."

Nancy said it was possible the person who left the visible print had not intended to. Furthermore, she suspected that if any substitution of a page had been made, it was the third sheet. "Peg, where is the will now?"

"A lawyer has it, but my father has a copy, even of the thumbprint."

18

"Good," said Nancy. "Would your dad let us see it?"

Peg nodded. "When I asked him if he'd mind my bringing it to the attention of the Detective Club, he said it would be a good idea. Nancy, he thinks you're an ace at solving mysteries."

Nancy smiled and urged that the members of the club hurry over to Peg's home. Her father was there and greeted the girls cordially. At Peg's request he brought out the copy of the will and laid it on the dining room table. "What have you figured out so far?" he asked.

"Not much, I'm afraid," Nancy replied. "Mr. Goodale, did you see the original?"

"Yes."

"Did you notice whether page three differed slightly from the others?"

"No, I didn't. And I don't believe the lawyer did, either."

Peg now picked up the copy. "Nancy, could you tell from this if there is a difference among the pages?"

Nancy looked carefully at each sheet. "The printing on page three is a shade lighter than the rest. It is possible that this page has been substituted for the original."

"What a clever deduction!" Karen exclaimed. "You've solved part of the mystery, Nancy. Now how about the thumbprint?"

Sue asked if it might belong to the man named in the will. Mr. Goodale shook his head. "That has already been checked out. The FBI has a record of Mr. Murphy's print, and this does not match."

Peg's face fell. "So our suspect is no longer a suspect," she said. "Nancy, what are we going to do?"

The sleuth smiled. "We're not going to give up. Let's examine the thumbprint more closely."

She took a magnifying glass from her pocket. The other girls pulled out theirs, and all gazed intently at the copy of the will.

"All I see are a lot of whirligigs," Peg said, giggling.

"They're *whorls*," Sue said. "And the man has a lot of broad vertical wrinkles on his thumb. Does that mean anything?"

"It could mean," Nancy replied, "that his hand is almost constantly in contact with water or some other liquid. Name occupations like that."

"Car washer," Sue replied.

"Dishwasher in a restaurant," Karen guessed.

"Laundry person," Bess offered.

"Bottling factory, like orange juice, or peaches, or cherries," George added.

"Black cherries," Honey said. "Remember, the print is pretty dark."

The others laughed, except for Nancy.

"What's your guess?" Mr. Goodale asked her, noticing she had become thoughtful.

"It may be far-fetched, but the suspect could work in a dye factory, in which case his fingers could be stained. If he perspired, he could make a dark print."

"The suspect could work in a dye factory," Nancy said.

Suddenly, Mr. Goodale jumped up. "Nancy, I believe you have found the guilty person!"

Everyone stared at him.

"The Murphys have a son, Selig," he explained. "He works in a dye factory. I'll call the lawyer and have this Selig Murphy investigated at once."

"Let us know what happens," the girls begged as the meeting of the Detective Club broke up.

Mr. Goodale promised to do so, but it was not until two days later that Peg gave the girls a report in the Drew living room. Selig Murphy had confessed. When his parents were discharged by Grandpa Goodale, they kept a key to the house. From time to time, they went there with Selig while Grandpa Goodale was in the hospital and no one was at home.

"But why?" Honey asked.

"The Murphys stole various pieces of silver jewelry—even furniture," Peg explained. "Things they felt he wouldn't miss. In looking through his desk one day, they came across the will. They took it home to change the names of the main beneficiaries. Selig rented a typewriter that matched the one that had been used to draw the will. He copied the original text, but substituted his parents' names on page three for those of my parents. Then he returned the revised will to the desk drawer."

"And all the while Selig was very nervous," Honey deduced, "and perspired freely, leaving a telltale thumbprint on the back of the substitute sheet!"

Peg nodded and everyone clapped.

"Nancy Drew, you're responsible for solving this mystery," Peg said. "My parents are really happy at the outcome."

"Don't forget," said Nancy, "you all helped."

"Even Selig." Peg grinned. "I'm certainly glad he left his thumbprint on the will. Without it, my parents never would have been able to prove that the document had been tampered with!"

## ACTIVITY

What kind of fingerprint do you have?

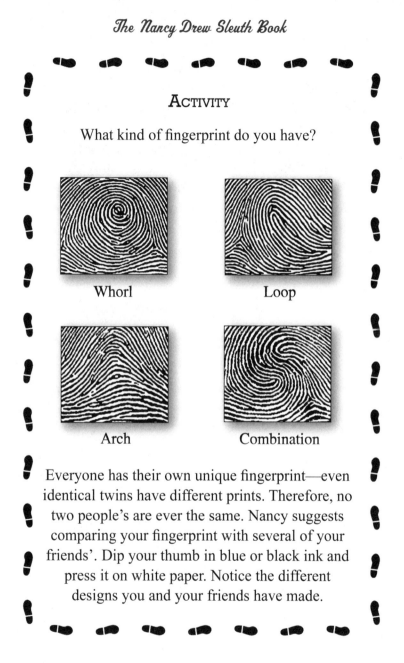

Whorl

Loop

Arch

Combination

Everyone has their own unique fingerprint—even identical twins have different prints. Therefore, no two people's are ever the same. Nancy suggests comparing your fingerprint with several of your friends'. Dip your thumb in blue or black ink and press it on white paper. Notice the different designs you and your friends have made.

# Chapter III

# Get the Fugitive
*Identification and Sleuthing*

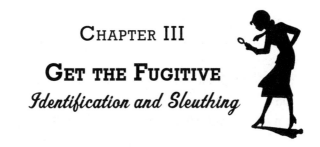

"WHAT an experience!" exclaimed Karen Carpenter, a charter member of Nancy Drew's Detective Club. "Tell us about it again, Martie, and don't leave anything out."

Martie Wagner was quite upset about what had happened to her while on an errand for her mother at Wright's Jewelry Store.

"No one was around," she reported, "so I waited and looked over the jewelry and silverware inside the glass counters. I didn't hear a sound, but suddenly a blindfold was tied across my eyes and a gag stuffed in my mouth! I tried hard to hit my attacker, but couldn't see and couldn't yell."

"So what did you do?" Sue Fletcher asked, her eyes wide with shock.

"I pulled the gag out, and worked and worked until I got the kerchief off my eyes. By this time my assailant had disappeared, and I didn't hear anything. For a second I thought a ghost must have done it."

"Didn't you yell then?" Peg asked.

Martie shook her head. "All I wanted to do was escape. As I rushed toward the front door an elderly man came in and asked me why I was running. Before I could answer, we both heard a groan coming from the back room.

"'What's that?' the man asked. 'Did you hurt somebody? Are you a thief?' I cried 'no, no,' and followed him to the back room. On the floor lay the store owner, bound, blindfolded, and gagged. It was awful!"

The other girls agreed, then urged Martie to go on with her story.

"There's not much more to tell. We freed Mr. Wright, and he called the police. The elderly man said he'd stay with him and advised me to go home, after the jeweler identified me as a friend of the family. He said I would be called later as a witness."

Nancy spoke up. "Didn't Mr. Wright tell his story?"

"Oh, yes," Martie said. "A tall, thin, masked man came into the store, forced him into the back room, and tied him up. Then the stranger must have grabbed what jewelry he could before he saw me."

Nancy said she would like to ask Martie some questions. "As you were having the blindfold put over your eyes, did the person who was doing it seem to be reaching down?"

*On the floor lay the store owner!*

"No, Nancy. The person's arms were on a level with my shoulders."

"Then perhaps the person wasn't tall like the thief Mr. Wright described, and that means there may have been two thieves together. Martie, do you remember more about the person who blindfolded you?"

After a few seconds' thought, Martie replied, "I recall a sweet odor."

"Perfume?" Honey Rushmore suggested.

When Martie nodded, Nancy suggested the person might have been a woman. "Any other clues?" she asked. "Did you notice your attacker's breathing?"

"Yes. It was heavy—as if the person had difficulty breathing."

"Perhaps the person was overweight," said Karen

"Good guess," Nancy agreed. She turned to Martie. "Is this the jacket you wore to the jewelry store?"

"Yes."

Nancy walked across the room and examined the tweed cloth. Then she picked up two curly red hairs from the back of the jacket. "I think your assailant had light red hair, probably short."

The club members stared at Nancy admiringly, and Martie said, "I do remember one other thing. The person had small feet."

"That means our suspect is probably a woman," said Nancy.

Martie continued. "While she was blindfolding me, one of her shoes was right alongside mine. It looked the same size as mine, so maybe she's my height. And I'd say she wore slacks and flat shoes. I could tell from the way she leaned against me."

Nancy remarked that the girls had made a pretty good identification of the mysterious attacker and thief. "Peg, would you please list them?"

Peg held up her fingers and checked off the clues. "The assailant is a woman, about Martie's height, is heavy, and gets short of breath. She has light red hair, probably short."

Karen put in, "And travels with a tall, thin man who is rather violent. Why don't we try to find them?"

"Good idea," said Honey. "But how do we start, Nancy?"

"By going to the street where Wright's is. We'll talk to people in nearby stores and anyone who might have been around when the robbery was taking place. Perhaps someone saw the couple come out of the jewelry shop."

"Maybe," Peg suggested, "we'll see the thieves!"

Nancy smiled. "I doubt it. They know the police will be after them. I'm sure they left quickly."

"Then how can we find them?" Sue asked.

Nancy said she did not expect to. "But we might pick up clues to the thieves' identity that the police haven't learned yet."

When the members of the Detective Club reached the area of the store, Nancy stopped suddenly. The girls looked at her inquiringly, then followed the direction in which she was glancing.

Martie asked, "You mean the cabbie at that taxi stand just beyond Wright's might have been here during the robbery?"

"Yes."

The girls walked over, and Nancy nudged Martie to ask him. When she did, he looked amused. "Are you playing detective?" he asked, then added, "I saw a man and a woman hurry out of Wright's. They got into a parked car and drove off. I didn't notice the license number, but the car was a dark sedan."

Nancy winked at Peg, who said, "Please tell us what the couple looked like."

As if to humor her, the cabdriver replied, "Well, the guy was tall and thin. The woman was shorter and had reddish hair." Then he laughed. "Do you think I'd make a good detective, too?"

Nancy smiled. "A very good one. Can you describe their faces, the shapes of their heads, and their ears?"

The cabbie looked at her with heightened interest. "You're really serious, aren't you? Well, I believe the man had a sharp face and a small goatee. His nose was sharp, too, and I'd even say his ears were pointed."

"That's a great description," Karen said. "Did you notice anything else?"

"Yes. I can tell you the guy was a mighty bad driver. His car was parked smack against the curb. He took off like a shot and sure gave the tires on the right side a beating. He scraped that curb so hard, I don't think the rubber's going to last long."

"Thanks a lot," Nancy said, and the girls walked away, whispering among themselves.

"What do we do next?" Peg wanted to know.

Nancy suggested going to police headquarters. "Our suspects may have police records. Also, Martie should tell her story to the authorities."

When the club members reached the building, the young detective introduced the girls to Chief McGinnis.

The officer greeted them and said, "If Nancy Drew is your teacher, and you are able to solve mysteries the way she does, someday you all may join the police department!"

The girls laughed, then Nancy asked Martie to tell her story. Martie did so and ended by saying, "I didn't get in touch with you, because Mr. Wright told me I'd be contacted later. I didn't see the suspects."

Chief McGinnis said, "By getting your club members to help, you have added a valuable bit of information to the case. We didn't know the masked man in Mr. Wright's store had a partner. So, she's a red-haired woman!"

Peg spoke up. "Do you know what the man looked like?"

"No," the chief admitted. "Mr. Wright couldn't give us a detailed description. And the thief must have worn gloves because he left no fingerprints."

"We got a lead from a cabdriver who saw the couple run out of the store and drive off in a dark sedan," Peg told the officer. There was a tone of mixed pride and teasing in her remark as she related their conversation with the taxi driver.

"Very good sleuthing," the chief said. He pushed a buzzer on his desk, and another officer walked in.

"This is Sergeant Walsh, ladies," Chief McGinnis said. "Mike, meet the Detective Club. They've brought some valuable clues about the Wright robbery. Will you see if there's a record of a tall, thin man with sharp features and slightly pointed ears whose partner is a heavyset woman with red hair?"

Mike left and returned a few minutes later with startling news. "The couple are husband and wife and are wanted in several cities for robberies. Apparently, they are now working the smaller towns."

"Send out an alarm for them at once," McGinnis ordered. Then he turned to the girls. "Thanks for your help. And good luck on your next mystery."

After the group had left, Nancy said, "Let's do some more inquiring." She led the club members back to Wright's, and they searched along the scraped curb for anything that might further identify the suspects or their sedan.

Martie pointed out the marks that indicated a car had scraped roughly along the curbing. They even noticed little pieces of rubber.

"That cabdriver wasn't exaggerating," Nancy said. "It's a slim chance, but let's hunt for a dark car with scraped tires on the right side." She hailed a limousine taxi, and all of the girls piled in.

"Where to?" the driver inquired.

For a moment, Nancy was embarrassed. Finally she said, "Just drive around until we spot a dark sedan with bad scrape marks on the right wheels."

"I know exactly where it is," the cabbie replied, much to the girls' surprise. "I passed it at the edge of town, where both tires blew out. I stopped to see if I could help, and the man said, 'No. I only have one spare. But there's a garage nearby. Ask them to send a tow truck here!'"

"What did the people in the car look like?" Martie asked.

"The man had a thin face and funny-looking ears. The woman with him had light red hair and was kind of heavy."

"That's the couple we're trying to find!" Martie blurted out. "They're thieves!"

"Don't let these people get away! They're wanted for assault and robbery!"

"What!" the driver exclaimed.

Nancy urged him to go to the garage as fast as possible. He set off with a roar and soon pulled up in front of the repair shop. The girls jumped out, and Nancy quickly paid their fare.

"Be careful!" the driver warned as the girls hurried toward the building.

A car was just being lowered from the right lift. The two suspected thieves were standing alongside it.

The instant Nancy saw them, she dashed into the office and said to the owner, "Don't let these people get away! They're wanted for assault and robbery at Wright's Jewelry Store. May I use your phone?"

"Go ahead," the man replied. "I'll keep the couple here."

Nancy dialed police headquarters and spoke to Chief McGinnis. When he heard her amazing report, he said, "We'll be there at once."

Within five minutes, three officers arrived, and the suspects were held while their car was searched. The jewelry found in it was identified by Mr. Wright, who had been hastily summoned. He also identified the mask worn by his attacker.

Martie took the telltale light red hairs from her purse. They matched the woman's hair perfectly. The couple was arrested and taken away in the police car.

## ACTIVITY

Nancy suggests that readers write down descriptions
of people they pass in the street or in a car.
Look for traits according to the following list.
Your observation skills will improve with practice.

Sex                     Ears
Ethnicity               Shape of head
Age                     Shape of face
Height                  Glasses
Weight                  Complexion
Build                   Scars or marks
Hair                    Tattoos
Eyes                    Any peculiarities
Nose

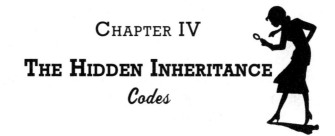

## CHAPTER IV

# THE HIDDEN INHERITANCE
## *Codes*

NANCY brought her three-legged childhood blackboard from the attic and set it up in the living room. She took a piece of chalk from a box, consulted a slip of paper in her left hand, then wrote:

WECANCERTAINLYN
OTEACOTEBY
THECOOING

A few minutes later, the members of her Detective Club began to arrive. In turn, each one asked, "What's that?"

"A code for you to figure out," Nancy replied. "Buried in a sentence is a name you know well. What does the sentence say, and what is the name hidden inside?"

The girls stared at the blackboard for several minutes. Each one finally said, "I give up."

Nancy smiled. "A good detective absolutely never gives up."

She asked the girls to take their notebooks and work on the puzzle. "Most codes are based on the transposition of letters or numbers," she said. "This one is based on letters."

She left the room for ten minutes. When the young detective returned, she asked, "Any luck?"

"A little," Peg spoke up. "The first line says, 'We can certainly,' but what's the *N* for?"

Nancy laughed. "How about hooking it to the beginning of the next line?"

Peg did. "The next word could be *note*."

"Good. Keep going."

Presently, Sue called out, "Note a cote. A cote's where you keep pigeons, isn't it?"

Nancy nodded. "So far you have, 'We can certainly note a cote.' What's next?"

"Ah, I know," Karen exclaimed. "Pigeons coo. The sentence is, 'We can certainly note a cote by the cooing.'"

The others clapped, then Peg asked, "How do we find the hidden name?"

Nancy suggested that the girls try using numerical relationships in the sentence this time, like perhaps the first letter in each word. "But that isn't the answer in this case, so try something else."

WE CAN CER TAINLYN
OTE A CO TE BY
THE CO DING

*"How do we find the hidden name?"* Peg asked.

At once the Detective Club members began to count on their fingers. After a while, Peg held up five fingers, and Nancy nodded.

"Girls," said Peg, "try every fifth letter."

They did, and called out in unison, "It's *Nancy!* The hidden name is Nancy!"

There was much laughter, and the girls remarked, "Well, what do you know?" "Pretty clever and tricky," and "How come we couldn't figure it out ourselves?"

When the noise subsided, Nancy said, "You just aren't used to codes, but don't worry—there's plenty more where that came from. This was just a teaser. Karen and I have a mystery for all of us to solve. She will tell you about it."

Karen stood up and showed the others a paper that looked as if words on it might be a sentence, but the message made no sense.

"This is a copy of a piece of paper my father found at the bank in the safe-deposit box of a Mr. Carvello who died. Dad is an executor and is trying to settle the estate. In the will, Mr. Carvello left everything to a children's home, but nothing of value has been found in his house except a few pieces of furniture. Since Mr. Carvello was reputed to be wealthy, this seems strange. But Dad did tell me the man was an eccentric."

Nancy asked, "Does your dad think this paper may contain a clue to something of value that's hidden?"

"He does," Karen replied. "He planned to take the message to a specialist in breaking codes, but he said if the members of our Detective Club wanted to work on it, he'd wait a couple of days."

"We'll certainly try," Nancy replied, and the other girls said, "You bet."

Nancy took the paper and copied the strange words on the blackboard.

FSSU CSI KZFPZAFX IXOZIB VG CZFQX CFSSI

Peg called out, "It looks like some foreign language!"

"It sure does," Martie agreed. "Nancy, how do we tackle this?"

"First, look for double letters. Then, figure out what double letters occur most frequently in words."

After several moments Honey said, "Not *AA*, except in 'baa, baa,' but that's not likely to be in a code. Say, how about *EE*?"

Nancy nodded, and Peg said, "Double *I* isn't usual, but double *O* is. And there's *BB* and *CC* and *DD* and *FF* and *GG* and *LL* and *MM* and *NN* and double *P* and—"

"You'd better try the vowels first," Nancy advised.

Karen was saying, "Feed, feel . . ."

Sue struggled with *BOO*. "Maybe book. *COO*—perhaps cool. Maybe fool, food . . ."

Nancy reminded the club members that she doubted the first *F* meant *F*, rather some other transposed letter.

Sue continued as she had started. *"GOO, LOO.* Maybe the word is *look!"*

"That's a clever guess," Nancy said. She wrote down the letters of the alphabet, one under the other. Then she put *S* next to *O, F* next to *L*, and wrote *U* alongside *K*.

Peg had another clue. "The last word has an *SS* for *OO*, and an *F* for an *L*. Could the word be *floor?"*

"Let's try it," said Nancy. "If it's correct, it would give us *C* for *F* and *F* for *L*, and *S* for *O,* and *I* for *R.*"

The girls were excited. Now it was easy to fill in *FALSE FLOOR.* Sure they were on the right track, each member worked diligently. Letter after letter was chalked on the board.

Suddenly, Peg cried out, "I think I can see the pattern!"

Nancy smiled. "I see it, too."

"I suppose I'm slow," Cathy said, "but I don't get it. Will you tell me?"

"It's the last letter of the alphabet, then the first," Peg explained. "Then comes the second to last and the second, the third to last and the third, and so on."

Peg slapped her forehead with her palm. "Of course! How could I have missed it?"

"It's quite confusing," Nancy admitted. "Just to get it all clear in our minds, let's write each code letter followed by the corresponding letter in the alphabet."

The girls did, and came up with the following columns:

| | | |
|---|---|---|
| Z = A | E = J | Q = S |
| A = B | U = K | J = T |
| Y = C | F = L | P = U |
| B = D | T = M | K = V |
| X = E | G = N | O = W |
| C = F | S = O | L = X |
| W = G | H = P | N = Y |
| D = H | R = Q | M = Z |
| V = I | I = R | |

When this was done, Nancy said, "Now let's see if we can decipher the mysterious message. Just write the corresponding letters underneath the code letters."

The girls did, and cried out in amazement.

FSSU  CSI  KZFPZAFX  IXOZIB  VG  CZFQT  CFSSI

LOOK  FOR  VALUABLE  REWARD  IN  FALSE  FLOOR

Karen jumped up. "I must tell my dad about this right away!"

Nancy said, "Ask him if we may go out to Mr. Carvello's mansion and try to find the false floor and the treasure!"

Karen called her father and talked for a long time. Then she hung up, smiling. "Dad was absolutely thrilled. Doesn't see how we broke the code so fast. He's leaving the front-door key at his office. He's sorry he can't wait for us, but he has to go to a business meeting. Says we'll need extra nourishment for our afternoon's work, so he's treating us all to lunch at the golf club. We'll take my station wagon."

Two hours later the girls reached Mr. Carvello's residence, and Karen let them in.

"What a gloomy place!" Cathy Chase exclaimed, discovering that the electricity had been turned off. "Imagine living here all alone!"

Nancy pointed out that the curtains were drawn.

"Let's open them," Cathy urged. "This place gives me the creeps the way it is."

The girls lifted shades and pulled back drapes. Instantly, the first floor became very attractive as sunlight fell on the rugs, furniture, and pictures.

The searchers began to turn back the carpeting and move the furnishings, hunting for a false floor. They went from room to room examining every inch, but found nothing.

Finally Peg stood up to stretch her back. "We've sure made a mess of this place, and yet haven't discovered the treasure." She sighed.

The others restored the furniture to the proper places and went to the second floor. Here it was difficult to work, as beds and bureaus were heavy to move. It took the girls over an hour to finish their search of the upstairs.

"And no false floor," Sue complained.

Nancy smiled. "A good detective never allows herself to be discouraged. Come on, let's try the third floor."

The Detective Club members climbed the steep steps. At the top they saw two bedrooms and an attic.

"My hunch is," said Nancy, "that these rooms won't give us a clue, but the attic may. Suppose two of you examine the bedrooms. The rest of us will check the attic."

It was soon evident that neither of the rooms contained a false floor, so all of the girls concentrated on the big, open attic. There were many trunks and boxes, and the place was cluttered. In order to examine the wooden floor beneath, the young detectives had to shift the objects around until their arms ached.

"Nancy, do you think Mr. Carvello might have meant the floor of a trunk?" Peg asked, rubbing her left shoulder.

"He could have. Let's find out."

Each trunk was turned upside down and tapped thoroughly. They proved to be solid.

"Guess again, Peg," Cathy teased.

"I'm all out of guesses. We've certainly covered this house from top to bottom!"

"With one exception," Nancy reminded her. "The cellar."

"Oh, no!" Sue groaned. "I'm exhausted!"

But she trooped down to the basement with the others, not wanting to admit defeat.

*Each trunk was turned upside down and tapped thoroughly.*

"That false floor had better be here," Karen declared, "or I'll never bother to decipher another code!"

A series of rooms made up the basement. First the club members entered a canned fruit closet, its shelves bare. The floor was solid cement. While the girls were busy examining a rec room, they suddenly noticed that Nancy was missing.

"Where'd she go?" Karen asked, and called her friend's name.

There was no answer! Worried, she and the others ran along the corridor calling the young detective and opening doors. Finally they came to a large door and had a hard time opening it. When it budged, they were relieved and surprised. Nancy stood inside!

"You gave us a real scare!" Karen said.

"I'm sorry," Nancy apologized. "But I found this refrigeration room—"

"This is the biggest freezer I've ever seen!" Sue giggled.

"It certainly is huge," Nancy agreed. "I had a sudden hunch that maybe the code meant the floor of a refrigerator or freezer, so I hunted for one. I walked in here and examined the box thoroughly, but found nothing. By the way, it's a good thing the power was turned off, or I'd be frozen by now."

"Icicle Nancy," Sue kidded.

"Girls," Nancy said suddenly, "I have another hunch. Look at what we're standing on!"

For the first time the others realized that the floor was a heavy, wooden slatted mat on top of cement.

Karen exclaimed, "The false floor! Oh, let's pick the mat up and see what's underneath!"

It took the combined strength of all to turn the mat up on end. They stared at what was underneath—a two-foot-square section set into the cement with a pull ring!

Karen tugged at it. At last, with Sue's help, she pulled up the slab of cement. Underneath lay a metal box. The girls lifted it out.

"This must contain the treasure!" Karen cried out. She tried to open the lid of the metal container, but it would not budge.

Everyone sighed in frustration, then Nancy spoke up. "Karen, maybe your dad has a key to this."

"Right. Let's take the box to his office."

The girls locked the house and left hurriedly in the station wagon. Mr. Carpenter had returned from his meeting and stared unbelievingly at the metal box when Karen set it on his desk. Quickly she told how the girls had solved the mystery.

"Please open it if you have a key," she begged.

Her father took a large bunch of keys from his desk drawer. "I hope one of these fits," he said. "I found them in Mr. Carvello's house, but they were not marked."

After several tries he picked a slender key that fit. There was a click of the lock, then he raised the lid.

"Money!" Karen cried out.

Bills were tied in bundles. Mr. Carpenter lifted them out one by one and asked the girls to count them. For several minutes no one spoke, then one by one the club members called out a sum.

Karen's father added them on a machine. Finally he exclaimed, "That's unbelievable! There is a hundred and fifty thousand dollars here!"

"And it's all for the children's home!" Karen exclaimed.

Her father looked at Nancy Drew. "This is an amazing bit of detective work."

She smiled and said, "There are very bright girls in our club."

"I still can't figure out why Mr. Carvello hid the money in the refrigeration room and left this complicated code for his executors to figure out!" Karen declared.

"As I told you before," Mr. Carpenter replied, "he was an eccentric person. Even though he was an engineer by profession, he was an expert on codes, which he studied as a hobby. He often helped the police with this type of thing."

Peg giggled. "Well, he certainly didn't help us! He went out of his way to make matters complicated."

"He must have known Nancy Drew was around to solve his puzzle!" Karen concluded.

## ACTIVITY

Nancy suggests that you and a friend make
up a code for writing secret messages to each other.
Remember that code letters often coordinate
to a letter in the alphabet.

Using what you've learned from the story,
figure out this confidential message:

Z WSSB BXJXYJVKX ZAQSFPJXFN GXKXI WVKXQ PH

To see if you've cracked this code, turn to page 152.

# CHAPTER V

## CHANGING SHOE PRINTS
### *Plaster Casts, or Moulages*

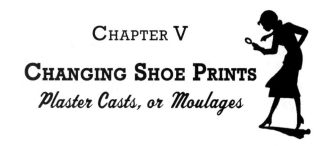

"SUE'S fifteen minutes late," Nancy remarked to the members of the Detective Club. "Were any of you in touch with her?"

"No," the girls responded.

Just then the telephone rang. Nancy hurried to answer it. The caller was Sue Fletcher, and she was quite excited.

"Please come downtown right away! There's a big fire! The neighbors think an arsonist set it. I found some shoe prints leading from the back door. Maybe we can find the person who set the fire!"

"Good idea," Nancy said. "We'll be right there. Where is it?"

"On the corner of Krum and Archer streets. It's a big, old white house. Hurry!"

Nancy hung up and gave the girls Sue's message. The club members jumped up and seconds later piled into Nancy's car. Soon they arrived at the scene of the fire.

The old dwelling was burning briskly. Sparks were flying in every direction. The ornate old-fashioned trim on the building was igniting and falling in flaming chunks to the ground.

Fire engines, pumpers, and a hook and ladder were already in action, with some of the firefighters manning hoses and others climbing to the upper floors. A sizable crowd of onlookers was held at a safe distance by police.

"Let's find Sue," Nancy suggested, and the girls circumvented the crowd to reach the back of the house.

Here, flames were bursting through broken windowpanes. Sue stood near a rear hedge watching in fascination.

"This is dreadful!" she said. "Can you imagine anyone setting fire to a beautiful old home like this?"

"No," Nancy spoke up, "or to any home. A person must be insane to do such a thing. What did the neighbors say, Sue?"

"The woman next door saw a figure in a long raincoat and a rain hat run out of the back door and go through the hedge over there. Soon afterward the fire broke out in several places at once. That's why she believes he set the fire."

"It was a man?" Peg asked.

"The neighbor thinks so," Sue replied.

Martie said thoughtfully, "Maybe the man was a burglar. But why he would bother to wreck the place afterward?"

"To make sure no clues are found," Peg replied. "Don't you think so, Nancy?"

Nancy smiled. "You're jumping to conclusions. You don't even know if the man was a burglar."

Her friends admitted this was true. But then why was the home set on fire?

"Let's begin by examining the shoe prints," Nancy suggested.

"They're funny!" Martie declared. "They don't match. Maybe the arsonist has a clubfoot and wears special shoes?"

"That's a good guess," Nancy agreed, "but why wouldn't the two resemble each other? These are totally different. One has a smooth sole and a corrugated heel and is smaller than the other, which has a rubber heel with a star on it and a corrugated rubber sole."

"What does it mean?" Karen asked.

Nancy shrugged, then said, "The Federal Bureau of Investigation has a complete record of the soles and heels of every pair of shoes manufactured in the United States."

"But how can you get these prints to the FBI in Washington, D.C.?"

Sue said, "You could photograph them."

*"The shoe prints don't match!" Martie declared.*

"That's true," Nancy agreed. "But you have to measure the length and width of each section—the front part, the arch, and the heel. These measurements must be sent along with the photographs."

Martie sighed. "Sounds like a lot of work." She was glancing at the house, and suddenly started to scream. "Oh!"

The others stared in the direction she pointed, and they cried out, too. A large, flaming cornice had broken loose from under the overhang of the roof and was hurtling toward the garden. Instinctively, the girls pushed through the hedge into a large flower bed on the other side. They were not a moment too soon. The cornice landed and split into hundreds of pieces, sending a shower of sparks high into the air.

"Maybe we shouldn't stay here," Peg said fearfully.

Nancy was calm now. "I'm sure we're safe on this side," she said. "And we should work on the footprints. Those in the garden are ruined, so we must pick up the ones over here. I'll dash home and get my camera and my moulage kit. You wait here."

As the young sleuth hurried off, Honey Rushmore asked, "What's a moulage kit?"

"It holds material for making a plaster cast of things like shoe prints," Peg replied.

Sue thought the girls should hunt for a good sample of the suspect's impressions for Nancy to use. It took them several minutes to locate a perfect right and left print in the soft earth, since their own were there, as well as those of another person, presumably the gardener.

Nancy arrived just as the club members made their decision. "They're excellent," she agreed. "Deep enough that we won't have to make a wall around the prints to keep the plaster from running over the sides."

She handed Sue the camera. "Since this is your case, how about you take the pictures? Snap most of them from above, and get as close as possible so every detail will show. Cathy, will you take the measurements? The rest of you can help me."

Nancy had received permission to park in the driveway of the house where the girls were working. She carried the moulage kit to the flower bed, set it on the ground, and opened it. Inside the box was a metal mixing bowl, a stirrer, and a spatula. Alongside lay a bag of quick-drying white plaster of Paris powder and a bottle of water.

"Martie, will you empty the powder into the bowl, and Peg, please pour the water in gradually. I'll stir."

In less than a minute, the plaster was ready. Nancy carefully dropped plaster into the right shoe print until it was half an inch thick, then gently patted it firm. Finally, she smoothed it with the spatula.

She now laid thin strips of wood over the cast as a base to turn the cast upside down on after it had dried. Before working on the left shoe print, the girls stopped to look at the snapshots Sue had taken.

"They're great!" Nancy praised her. "Take some more at different angles."

She prepared a new batch of plaster and, in a few minutes, finished the cast of the suspect's left shoe print.

"As soon as these dry," Nancy said, "we'd better follow the stranger's trail."

When the moulages were ready, they were carefully laid in the trunk of Nancy's car. Then she put the kit on the floor of the backseat before the girls set off on their sleuthing. The prints led to the next block, then veered off into a stretch of woodland. A quarter of a mile farther on, they stopped abruptly.

"Now what do we do?" Karen asked.

Nancy did not reply. Instead, she looked carefully around the area. The undergrowth was thick, and it was difficult to detect any marks on the ground. Suddenly she called out, "Come here, everyone! Tell me if you see anything unusual."

The club members gazed around. Finally Sue said, "The bushes have been trampled."

"Yes. Let's see where the broken path leads."

As the girls climbed across the tangled mass Martie cried out, "Ouch! There are briars in here!"

Sue giggled. "A good detective never lets a few briars stand in her way."

Her friends laughed, then plunged ahead. When they reached the far side of the wooded area, the girls stopped and searched again for the uneven shoe prints. They saw none, but presently Peg, who was in the lead, exclaimed, "I just noticed a different set. They match!"

Everyone hurried forward to study her new discovery. Nancy remarked, "They're small enough to belong to a woman."

"Maybe the suspect met a woman here?" Karen said.

"Then what did he do with his own shoes? Carry them and walk in his stocking feet?"

The girls searched for footprints, but found no extra set. Nancy suggested that the arsonist could have changed shoes at this point. "He probably used the phony ones to go to the house to set the fire. He might even have slipped them on over his regular shoes. Sue, why don't you take some snapshots of these new prints, and then we'll see where they lead us."

As soon as Sue had finished, the young detectives continued their search. It was reasonably easy to follow the trail across fields to a farmhouse with the name STEDMAN on the mailbox. Nancy went to the back porch and knocked on the kitchen door. A little girl answered.

"Hello," the young detective said. "My name is Nancy. What's yours?"

"Josie."

"Is your daddy or your brother at home?"

"Not my daddy. He's at work. My make-believe brother is. But you can't see him. He's taking a bath. Did he come home a mess!"

Nancy's eyes roved around the porch. On a hook hung a man's raincoat and hat. In one corner she spotted a pair of pants and a shirt that reeked of gasoline. Underneath lay two unmatched shoes. Did they belong to the suspect? Had he started the fire with gasoline?

Nancy's pulse was racing, but she smiled calmly at the little girl. "Why do you say he's a 'make-believe brother'?"

"'Cause he's not my real brother. Mommy and Daddy brought him here from some school. I don't like him. He does bad things instead of his chores, like going off without telling anybody. And he teases me. He's mean!"

Nancy asked Josie if her mother was at home.

"Yes, but she's sleeping. She works nights."

There was a long pause, then Nancy asked if she might use the telephone. "My friends and I took a long walk, and we'd like to ride back. If it's okay, I'll call my daddy to come and get us."

"Go ahead. Mommy won't mind." Josie led Nancy to the wall phone in the dining room.

The young sleuth dialed her father's private number. When he answered, she said, "This is Nancy Polly. The girls and I are at a farmhouse on Chester

Road. The name is Stedman. Could you pick us up? Hurry, please! We left my car in town at Krum and Archer streets. And thanks a lot."

She hung up and turned to the little girl. "You're so sweet. I'll go and tell my friends we'll get a ride home."

Nancy went outside and whispered to the members of the Detective Club, "I think we've cornered the arsonist. Dad's coming with the police."

"What!" Sue exclaimed. "Tell us about it."

"I will, but first we must be sure the suspect won't guess what's going on and try to escape. You girls pretend to be strolling around the house and guard all the entrances. If anyone comes out, yell."

Within fifteen minutes, Mr. Drew and a detective arrived in Nancy's car. Behind them was a coupe with two plainclothes policemen. Nancy hurried to meet them and reported the girls' discovery.

"I made moulages of the strange unmatching shoe prints," she added. "Those shoes and some clothes smelling of gasoline are on the back porch. Suppose I show Dad where the articles are, and he can bring them to you."

After Mr. Drew had left the porch, Nancy knocked on the door again. Josie opened it. Nancy requested that the wide-eyed child awaken her mother gently and ask her to come downstairs to meet the visitors. Josie hurried out of the kitchen

*"This is Nancy Polly. Could you pick us up? Hurry, please!"*

and returned five minutes later with a sweet-faced woman. By this time the police had compared the moulages with the shoes. They matched perfectly!

Mr. Drew was introduced to Josie and her mother. "Is your son at home, Mrs. Stedman?" he inquired.

"Yes," she replied. "Why are you asking?"

"He's suspected of arson," the lawyer said and, in a low voice, related the circumstances. "The house that burned down belongs to Judge Ryman. Does that name mean anything to you?"

The woman nodded, and tears came to her eyes. "After Bobby was found guilty of stealing, Judge Ryman sentenced him to a reform school. My husband and I offered to take him here on a trial basis. He's a good farmworker but is absent a lot. Oh, this is dreadful. Poor Bobby!"

At this moment the group heard footsteps on the stairs, and a dark-haired youth of seventeen appeared, dressed in a clean shirt and jeans. Without waiting for an introduction, he cried out, "Where are my clothes and shoes?"

"Calm down, Bobby," said Mrs. Stedman gently. She looked straight at him. "The police have proof that you set Judge Ryman's house on fire."

Bobby screamed, then became defiant. "I don't know what you're talking about."

By this time the officers and the rest of the Detective Club had come into the kitchen. Detective

Closter explained how a neighbor had seen a figure wearing a raincoat and rain hat running from the rear door of Ryman's house, and how the girls had made moulages of his unmatched shoe prints and followed them to the farm.

"If I'm not mistaken," he said, "you took off the unmatched shoes in the woods and are now wearing the pair you had on underneath."

Sue opened her handbag and showed several photographs to the detective. "I made pictures," she said.

Detective Closter looked at her admiringly. "Good work." Then he turned to Bobby. "Let me see the bottoms of your shoes!"

Despite his protest, the young man was made to sit down, and his soles were examined. The pattern matched that in the pictures perfectly!

Bobby, realizing that he had been caught, flopped down into a chair and covered his eyes with his hands. "I just had to do it!" he cried. "I hate that judge. He sent me away! He deserved to lose his house."

Mrs. Stedman put an arm around the boy. "I suppose you'll have to go back to reform school. It's too bad you didn't keep to the straight path you started to follow here. Hatred never pays off, and retaliation only gets you into trouble."

"How right you are, Mrs. Stedman," Detective Closter said. "Come along with us, Bobby."

Mr. Drew went with the police and their prisoner. The girls climbed into Nancy's car and on the way home talked excitedly about the case they had solved.

"Nancy, how did you manage to tell your father to bring the detectives?" Sue asked.

Nancy smiled. "Dad and I have a little code we use. Whenever I want him to bring the police, I use a false middle name. I said, 'This is Nancy Polly.'"

"Pretty clever," Sue remarked, and grinned at her teacher.

## ACTIVITY

Nancy suggests that you compare the soles of your shoes with those of your friends and take note of the many differences that can be helpful in identifying their imprints. Whether you have running shoes, boots, heels, or basic flats—all can leave a print in the soft earth. Shoe prints can be extremely helpful in catching a suspect.

# CHAPTER VI

# AIRPORT CHASE

## *Observation*

AS the members of the Detective Club walked into the Drew living room, they found Nancy wearing dark glasses.

"Oh, did something happen to your eyes?" Sue asked worriedly.

Nancy shook her head. "This is part of today's lesson. You girls know me pretty well. What color are my eyes?"

"Blue," Peg said.

"Gray," Karen guessed.

Cathy shrugged. "Green?"

There was a pause. Nancy smiled. "The only thing you seem to remember is that they're not brown." She took off the dark glasses, and the girls stared at her.

"I was right. They're blue!" Peg called out.

"Today," said Nancy, "we're going to talk about being observant so that from one quick glance at a person, you can describe him or her accurately."

Honey sighed. "I'd need three pairs of eyes to do that."

Nancy set up her blackboard and drew the outline of a human body, putting in dots for eyes, nose, and mouth.

"You'll notice that the geometric shape of this figure, like all human bodies, is a triangle," she said. "The head is the most important part. The body has two of almost everything, so in nearly every case, it can be divided in half when you're making your observation."

Cathy heaved a sigh. "I'm glad of that. It seems to be less work."

"Make a list of the following for the head," Nancy went on, and chalked a column on the blackboard.

1. Shape
   a. Egg-shaped
   b. Round
   c. Flat
   d. High crown
   e. Tilted forward, or backward, or to the side
   f. Bulging in front or back

Nancy went on, "Now describe the ears." She wrote the following categories on the board:

2. Ears
   a. Round
   b. Triangular
   c. Rectangular

"Now let's talk about hair," said Nancy. "Not only the color but the texture. Is it—?" She turned to the blackboard and wrote:

3. Hair
   a. Curly
   b. Straight
   c. Wavy
   d. Kinky

"Next come the eyes," said Nancy. She drew a line from one eye to the margin. "Get out your notebooks, girls, and copy what we have so far."

While they did this she wrote in the margin:

4. Eyes
   a. Color
   b. Shape: oval, round, almond
   c. Size

    d. Bloodshot
    e. Excessive blinking

The next facial feature to be studied was the forehead. Nancy wrote the following descriptions on the blackboard:

5. Forehead
    a. Bulging
    b. Prominent
    c. Wrinkled

The girls jotted this down, then Sue asked, "How about the shape of the face?"

"That's next," Nancy said, and wrote:

6. Shape of face
    a. Round
    b. Oval
    c. Broad
    d. Long

"That's easy," Karen remarked. "You can't change the shape of a person's face, because of the skull structure."

Nancy said, "But look carefully for scars, cuts, rashes, and of course beards and mustaches. Does the beard nearly cover the face, or only partially? Is it well trimmed? Is the mustache long or short? Does it match the beard and hair?"

Peg groaned as she took notes. "This lesson is a big order. I don't see how I can remember all these things."

Nancy chuckled. "We haven't finished yet. Peg, how many kinds of eyebrows are there?"

"Heavy, skimpy." She thought a moment. "Long, short—I give up."

Martie raised her hand. "Straight and arched."

"I know a couple," Sue called out. "Slanted, plucked."

"What about color?" Nancy asked. "Is it different from the hair, beard, or mustache?"

Sue giggled. "My eyebrows are darker than my hair."

"Now we come to the nose and mouth," Nancy went on. "Noses certainly come in many varieties: short, medium, long, straight, tilted, hooked, thick, or thin. Look for injuries—a scar, or a nose that's deformed from an accident, like in football, baseball, hockey, soccer, or boxing."

Karen spoke up. "Or just by getting into an ordinary fight with another person. My brother got his nose broken and had to have cosmetic surgery to fix it."

Nancy nodded, then mentioned the mouth. She suggested that the girls describe as many shapes as they could think of.

Honey's eyes lit up. "The biggest one belongs to a clown. Wouldn't that be a great disguise for someone? Nobody could identify the person behind the makeup."

"I can think of the opposite," said Peg. "A rosebud-sized mouth. And how about thin lips and thick lips."

"And notice the teeth," Nancy added. "Are they real or artificial, white or discolored, and are there spaces between any of them?"

Sue added, "You wouldn't see that if the suspect was running away from you."

"True," Nancy replied, "but sometimes you might be spying and have a good chance to make note of these points."

She stood up. "Now let's go and describe some real people."

"Where?" Karen asked.

"The River Heights Airport. It's a busy place with thousands of incoming and outgoing travelers."

"Sounds great!" Sue exclaimed. "Maybe we can catch a villain!"

Excitedly, the Detective Club members set off in Nancy's car. Twenty minutes later they reached the airport, which was alive with activity. After they parked, the girls went into the main building. A man banged his heavy suitcase against Sue as he dashed past her, but did not apologize.

"You have a nerve!" she muttered.

He turned for a second, and she glimpsed an

angular face with a square-set jaw and piercing black eyes.

Just then a very stout woman wearing a shawl over her head and shoulders hurried past the group.

"What did you notice about her?" Nancy asked.

The girls looked at one another.

"She was heavy," Karen said. "But what else?"

Their teacher smiled. "The woman had short curly hair and sunken cheeks, as if she had no teeth. She had small hands and feet, and wore bedroom slippers."

"Nancy," said Peg, "you're positively too much for me. But here comes an elderly man. Let's see if we can describe him better."

As the gentleman passed the bench where the club members had seated themselves, he smiled. After he was gone, the girls compared notes.

"He had gray hair," Sue said, "and blue eyes. A long thin neck, and long legs. He wore a gray suit and black shoes. His hair was short, straight, and thick."

"That's much better," Nancy commented. "Keep your eyes open."

A flight had arrived at gate 1, and a group of people walked down a corridor toward the girls' bench. They all kept a normal pace except for one young woman who elbowed her way through the crowd at a fast clip. She held a beaded clutch purse in one hand and a large shopping bag in the other.

At once Nancy thought, *That's an expensive purse, probably imported, and my guess is there's a lot of money in it.*

The young woman's plain dark blue suit and tailored blouse were not the appropriate attire to accompany such a purse. It was definitely meant to be carried with evening clothes.

"Watch that woman," Nancy directed her companions.

"How can I?" Sue complained. "She's running fast."

"She's probably trying to make a connecting plane," Karen observed. "She's turning toward gate three."

"She's having trouble running while wearing her high heels, too," Honey added.

"What about her hair, eyes, nose, and mouth?" Nancy asked.

"She has big lips and plenty of lipstick," Martie replied.

None of the club members could tell the color of the stranger's eyes, but they agreed that her hair was dark brown. They were still discussing her when, suddenly, a woman's shrill cry rang through the terminal.

"I've been robbed! Quick, somebody catch the thief!"

*My guess is there's a lot of money in that purse,*
*Nancy thought.*

Nancy and her friends hurried toward the distressed passenger.

"What does the thief look like?" Karen asked the elderly woman.

"I don't know! Suddenly, I missed my beaded black purse. It must have happened while we were coming off the plane."

Instantly, Nancy thought of the young woman in the blue outfit. Before she could say anything, a guard joined the group and asked if he could be of help. After hearing the story, he asked, "Did anyone see a person snatch Mrs. Allen's purse?"

"No!" a passerby replied.

"Are you a police officer?" Nancy asked. "Do you have the authority to make arrests?"

"Yes. Why?"

"I think we have a lead. Will you and Mrs. Allen please follow us? We saw a woman with a purse just like Mrs. Allen described."

The guard looked surprised. "You did?"

"Yes. If we hurry, I'm sure we'll catch her in time."

The Detective Club members started off, with the guard close at their heels. Mrs. Allen could not keep up the pace and fell behind. The guard turned back, but she begged him to go ahead with the girls.

Soon the group rushed up to the metal detector at gate 3. The guard asked the attendant if she had noticed a young woman in a blue suit carrying a beaded purse and a large shopping bag.

"I noticed a woman who fits your description, but she had no purse."

"She probably hid it in the shopping bag," Honey spoke up.

"No doubt," the guard said, and quickly explained the situation. The attendant waved the group through the gate, and they hurried on.

The last passengers were just boarding. The guard asked the stewardess to delay takeoff while his group hunted for the suspect. She telephoned the pilot, and within seconds he appeared. When he heard the story, the pilot said to Nancy, "Point her out. We'll get to the bottom of this!"

Nancy led the way down the aisle. The other girls followed behind the pilot and the guard.

The passengers looked up in surprise and craned their necks as the group went by. Toward the rear of the plane, Nancy suddenly stopped. She had found the young woman sitting next to the cruel-looking man who had banged his bag into Sue in the terminal!

"There she is," Nancy whispered to the men, and her friends nodded in agreement.

The guard leaned over and asked the suspect if she had a black beaded purse.

"Of course not!" the young woman snapped.

"May I see the bag you are carrying?"

"No. It's none of your business!"

The guard showed his police badge. "I want to see it."

At this point her companion spoke up. "Listen, this lady's got rights!"

"I have a whole group of witnesses who saw her with a black beaded purse that may be stolen," the guard replied evenly.

There was a disturbance in the background as Mrs. Allen pushed her way forward. "I own the stolen purse and everything in it! Give it to me at once!"

She and the suspect glared at each other. Then to everyone's amazement, the woman began to cry. "Yes, I have it. I don't want to go to jail. He—he"—she looked at her companion—"he made me do it!"

"What are you talking about?" the man bellowed. "I don't even know you!"

The guard looked at him intently. "Ah, but I recognize you! You're called Sneaky-Eyed Pete and were in prison for smuggling diamonds, and you escaped. The two of you had better come along with me."

The couple did not budge, but Mrs. Allen did. Pushing the guard aside, she reached down and swooped up the woman's shopping bag. She rummaged inside and drew out a beautiful beaded black purse.

"This is mine!" she cried out triumphantly, and unsnapped it. "My money's still in it, and so are the diamonds. My husband is a jeweler, and I bought them for him."

"I don't want to go to jail. He made me do it!"
the woman cried out.

"Where?" the guard inquired.

"A dealer in New York."

After glancing at the stones, the guard said, "I'm inclined to believe that those diamonds are part of a shipment stolen in Holland and smuggled into this country."

"What!" Mrs. Allen was shocked. "You mean I bought stolen merchandise?"

"Perhaps not," the guard calmed her. "Don't worry about it. But give me the name of the dealer, and the police will investigate it and let you know."

The pilot now conferred briefly with the guard, then said, "It's past takeoff time. Will all of you please disembark?"

The two men forced the thief and the smuggler to unstrap their seat belts and go with the guard.

"I'll call for another officer to help you," the *pilot offered as the group walked toward the front of the plane.

"I can't thank you enough," Mrs. Allen said gratefully to the girls. "You certainly have sharp eyes."

The club members smiled, and Nancy said she hoped Mrs. Allen would have no trouble recovering her money from the New York dealer if the diamonds had been smuggled. She said good-bye to the woman, who followed the prisoners and the guards into the security office. Then the girls left the terminal and walked to the parking lot.

"Wow!" Sue exclaimed as they climbed into the car. "And I was only kidding when I said we might catch a villain!"

Nancy chuckled. "We didn't only catch one, we caught two!"

## Activity

Nancy suggests that you play detective-for-the-day and go to your local mall or movie theater and observe people's traits. Write down your notes and observations of passersby. Always remember to be subtle and try not to stare . . . too hard.

# CHAPTER VII

# THE QUEEN'S CAMEO
## *Lost and Found*

"I HAVE a great mystery for us to solve!" said Honey Rushmore as the Detective Club members met at Nancy Drew's home. "There's only one problem. The mystery is a year old."

"A year is a long time," Nancy said with a chuckle. "But tell us, what is it all about?"

"My mother took a trip last July. She was wearing a valuable cameo that was very old and had once belonged to a queen."

"A queen's possession?" Peg asked in awe. "How did your mother get it?"

"I really don't know," Honey replied. "But I remember as a child I was never allowed to touch the cameo because it was so valuable."

"What's the mystery?" Karen interrupted impatiently.

"Sometime after Mother boarded the sleeper train back to River Heights," Honey went on, "she lost the pin. She has no idea whether it came off her dress in the station, on the train, or in the street. When she arrived home, she discovered it was gone."

Sue wanted to know whether Mrs. Rushmore had been in touch with the police.

"Oh, yes," Honey answered. "They made a search of the station and the train, but they didn't find the cameo. Then Mother contacted her insurance company, and they searched, too. But still the pin did not turn up. Finally the insurance company paid her what they considered it was worth. But Mother's convinced that its value was at least ten times that much. She feels very bad about the loss because the brooch had been in her family a long time."

Cathy sighed. "If the police and the insurance people couldn't find the cameo, it seems to me there isn't much chance we can."

Nancy smiled. "Don't forget that the members of this Detective Club never give up. I classify this case under Lost and Found. I'll give you some hints on how to go about the sleuthing. First of all, did the police and insurance company go to all the pawnshops and fences in this area?"

"What are fences?" Sue asked.

Nancy explained that these were little-known places where people take stolen property to be sold illegally. "Such stores differ from legitimate pawnshops, where a person can leave an item in exchange for cash. The pawnbroker will not sell it for a certain length of time and will return it to the owner when he or she pays back the money with interest."

Honey assured the girls that pawnshops had been investigated. "I don't know about fences, and I don't believe my mother would. But I'm sure the police and the insurance company must."

"Why does your mother want to look for the cameo now?" Peg inquired.

"She saw a similar pin in a jewelry shop downtown," Honey explained. "It was priced much higher than what Mother had received from the insurance company. Now, suddenly, she wants to try finding it again and has given us the job."

"That's very flattering," Nancy remarked. "We'll certainly do our best."

"But where do we start?" Martie asked.

Nancy said she would like to hear more about Mrs. Rushmore's train trip. "Honey, what car was your mother in? How often did she go to the dining car? Did she leave her own car for any other reason than to eat?"

"I have no idea," Honey said.

"Do you think we could talk to your mother, if she's at home?"

"Oh, she's home," Honey replied. "She was hoping you would take the case and said she would wait to find out."

Nancy brought out her car, and the club members piled in. They reached the Rushmore house a few minutes later.

Honey's mother greeted the girls with a smile. "I just knew you'd agree to look for my brooch," she said.

"Yes," Nancy replied. "We'd like to try."

After the girls were seated in the living room, she said, "Mrs. Rushmore, we want to ask you a few questions. First of all, what was the name of your sleeping car?"

"Mount Rushmore. It was such an amazing coincidence. That's probably why I can still remember it."

Honey's mother went on to say that she had gone to the dining car once during her journey, but other than that had not left the sleeper.

Nancy asked whether anyone in the dining car had remarked about her cameo.

Mrs. Rushmore smiled. "Yes, now that you ask me, I remember. I sat across the table from a charming woman. She admired the pin and thought it was quite unique. She had never seen one like it."

"Then," Nancy concluded, "we can rule out the possibility that you lost your cameo getting on the train."

Mrs. Rushmore nodded.

Sue spoke up. "Did you talk to anyone else during your trip?"

Mrs. Rushmore thought a moment, then replied, "No. I read most of the time. There weren't many passengers on the train, and no one sat near me."

"Were you jostled at any time, including when you got on and off the sleeper?" Nancy inquired.

"No. Not that I remember."

"After arriving in River Heights," Cathy said, "how did you go home?"

"Our car was parked at the station. And it was carefully inspected, of course. The pin was not in it."

"From what you've told me," Nancy said, "I think the cameo was lost rather than stolen."

"Why?" Honey wanted to know.

"If a thief had taken the pin, he was probably exclusively a jewel thief. I think only a knowledgeable jewel thief would have recognized the cameo's value. And the police had plenty of time to track him down in the past year. They have a record of known jewel thieves and their fences. Also, the fact that few people were on the train and you don't remember being jostled suggest that you probably lost the brooch."

"But then why wasn't it found?" Mrs. Rushmore asked.

"I don't know," Nancy said. "If you'll excuse me for a moment, I'd like to call my dad. There's something I want to do, and he can help us."

Honey directed her to the hall telephone, and Nancy dialed her father's number. When Mr. Drew answered, she said, "Dad, I'm working on a case that has to do with sleeping cars. Don't I recall that several of them are in the railroad yard of River Heights? We're looking for one called Mount Rushmore. Could you find out if it's there and, if so, arrange for the Detective Club to investigate it?"

Mr. Drew chuckled. "I'll be glad to, Nancy. Are you working on an interesting mystery?"

"We are," Nancy replied, and told her father about it. Then she gave him the Rushmores' phone number and hung up.

She returned to the living room and told the others about her hunch. Since Nancy was known to have good hunches about solving mysteries, the girls were not surprised. For the next ten minutes they discussed the case, then the phone rang.

Nancy hurried to answer it and was delighted to hear her father's voice. "Any news?" she asked.

He said he had good news. The Mount Rushmore sleeper was indeed in the railroad yard. "It's in the back where the old cars are kept that are only used in emergencies. I got permission for you to inspect it. Go to the office and see Mr. Vasey. He'll be glad to open the car for you and let you look around."

"Thanks, Dad," said Nancy. "We'll go right now."

Two automobiles were used this time, since Honey's mother wanted to come along. Nancy led the way to the railroad yard. She and Mrs. Rushmore parked, then the detectives walked to the freight station. Mr. Vasey, a pleasant, gray-haired man, greeted them in his office.

"You're Nancy Drew's group?" he asked.

Nancy nodded. "My father made arrangements with you to let us search the Mount Rushmore sleeper."

"Correct. I'll take you there myself." He turned to Mrs. Rushmore. "I understand you rode in that particular car a year ago and lost a valuable cameo."

"That's right."

Mr. Vasey said he was sorry and hoped they would find the pin, although he knew the car had been thoroughly searched at that time.

He spoke to his assistant, then said to the visitors, "Follow me."

Mrs. Rushmore and the girls trailed after him through the railroad yard, around cars, and along several aisles. Honey remarked that she had never seen so many tracks in her life. Finally they reached the car they were looking for. Mr. Vasey unlocked the door for them.

"When you finish your work, just pull the door shut," he said. "It will lock itself."

He walked off, and the Detective Club entered the sleeper with Mrs. Rushmore. The girls hurried along the aisle with facing seats on each side and hidden beds under bulging partitions above them. They took in every detail of the interior.

"This car is really old," Peg remarked. "The wood is beautiful, and look at all those decorations! You don't see any of that in modern railroad cars."

Nancy asked Mrs. Rushmore whether she had slept in an upper or lower berth.

"A lower," Honey's mother replied. "As I told you, there weren't many people on the train, and as far as I remember, only a few of the upper berths were used."

Nancy said, "Then that eliminates our having to look in the upper area."

Honey asked her mother which of the seats she had occupied.

"I'm not sure," Mrs. Rushmore replied, "but I know it was on the right side, behind the engine, and about halfway down."

Nancy suggested that the club members divide up for a search. Some of them should look on the floor under the seats; others could inspect the seats themselves.

Eagerly the group set to work. Several of them chose seats near the middle of the right side and tugged and pulled until they got the cushions up. The girls were doing exactly what the porters do, making them into beds.

"Anybody want to take a nap?" Karen quipped.

Peg answered, "I never sleep without sheets and a pillow, and I don't see any."

"They're probably kept in the upper berths, which are closed in the daytime," Nancy said.

"Where did the passenger occupying the upper berth sit?" Martie asked.

"In the seat facing the one Mrs. Rushmore had," Sue replied.

The search went on for some time, but nothing was found. Apparently, the car had been thoroughly swept and vacuumed.

Honey was disappointed. "I was hoping so much that we'd find Mother's cameo," she said.

Nancy urged her not to be discouraged. "We've only started!" she pointed out.

Just then an elderly African American man walked into the car. He had a round, pleasant face and curly gray hair.

When Mrs. Rushmore saw him, she exclaimed, "Oh, you're Kalef. You were my porter while I was on a trip last year."

The man shook hands with her. "Indeed, I was," he said. "And I remember you. You're Mrs. Rushmore—one of the nicest ladies I've ever helped."

"Thank you," Mrs. Rushmore said, and introduced the girls. "Are you on another train now, Kalef?" she asked.

"No. As a matter of fact, the trip with you was the last one I made. I've been working in the office ever since."

Kalef went on to say that he had asked to serve this particular car because he had been born near Mount Rushmore. "That's why I remember your name," he told Honey's mother. "Every time I get a chance to see this old car, I walk up and down the aisle. It reminds me of my boyhood and my days as a porter."

"Did you know I lost my valuable cameo on that trip?" Mrs. Rushmore asked.

"Yes. I'm sorry about that. The police interrogated everyone who had been in the Mount Rushmore sleeper, and so did the insurance people. But we didn't find your pin."

"Is there anyone else who might know something about it?" Nancy asked. "Anyone who was in the car after you arrived in River Heights, but before the police came?"

Kalef scratched his head. "River Heights was the last stop. But now that you mention it, someone did come in for a moment."

"Someone you knew?"

"Yes. I know him well. He's one of the switchmen out in the freight yard." Kalef paused, then added, "But if you're thinking that he's a thief, I'm sure you're wrong."

"But he might give us a clue," Nancy said. "Would you mind taking us to him?"

"I'll be glad to," Kalef said.

They left the car, pulling the door shut to lock it.

"Now, you be careful," the man warned. "This is a dangerous place. Be sure to look in all directions."

The girls promised to and set off with him.

Suddenly Kalef stopped short. "I just had an idea. Once a year they have an auction over in the warehouse. It's for unclaimed articles lost on trains or in the station. Today they're having one. Maybe your cameo is there, Mrs. Rushmore, and you could claim it!"

"The police and the insurance company asked the Lost and Found department last July," Mrs. Rushmore replied. "It had not been turned in."

Kalef shrugged and went on at a fast pace. He was ahead of the group when he disappeared behind another car. As the detectives hurried to catch up to him Peg suddenly screamed. "Look out!"

A trainman's work car was coming toward them at high-speed. To the girls' dismay, it was switched onto the very tracks they were walking on!

"Oh!" Martie cried out. She seemed frozen to the spot.

Nancy grabbed her hand and yanked the girl along with her. "Jump!" she yelled.

The others leaped across the track. They were none too soon. The conductor of the work car had seen them, but too late to brake to a stop. If the girls had not moved quickly, they would have been run over!

"Oh, dear!" Mrs. Rushmore exclaimed. "I had no idea there would be such danger!"

"It's my fault," Nancy told her. "I promised we'd all be careful."

By this time Kalef had run back. He looked in horror when he realized what might have happened and was about to argue with the conductor of the work train, but Nancy cut him short.

"Never mind. Take us to see the switchman, please."

Again the group followed Kalef, but now they looked in all directions before proceeding. A few minutes later, he led them to the switchmen's tower. A tall, blond fellow was just coming down the iron steps.

"Hi, Rogers!" Kalef called out. "Some folks here want to see you."

The man stared at the group in puzzlement. "They want to see me? Why?"

"To ask you a couple of questions."

Nancy waited for Mrs. Rushmore to speak, but when she said nothing, the young sleuth smiled at the switchman. "We'll only keep you a minute. We're the Detective Club. We've been spending all morning trying to find a piece of jewelry that was lost a year ago in the Mount Rushmore sleeper. Kalef said that you had briefly been in the car before the police and insurance company searched it. Do you by any chance remember seeing a cameo brooch?"

The man was thoughtful for a moment. "Wait a minute. That rings a bell—yes. I picked one up from the floor. Can't remember when or what car it was. But it could have been about a year ago. Put it in my pants pocket and forgot all about it. Weeks later my

*A trainman's work car was coming at high speed toward the girls!*

wife found it when she took the pants to the cleaner. I took it over to the Lost and Found department."

"It might have been my cameo!" Mrs. Rushmore said excitedly.

"If you hurry to the warehouse where the auction is," Rogers said, "you might be able to get hold of it. I had no idea that it was worth anything, or I'd have turned it in right away. I'm sure the police asked Lost and Found for it at the time. Oh, I hope you'll get your pin back!"

Nancy asked where the warehouse was.

"It's too dangerous for you to get there crossing the tracks," Kalef said. "You'd better go back to the street and drive down. Stay alongside the fence until you come to a road that leads right to the warehouse. You can't miss it."

The group thanked the men and dashed off. In a few minutes they arrived at the auction. To their dismay, many people were walking out of the building with packages under their arms.

"I hope the auction isn't over yet!" Honey said worriedly.

The girls and Mrs. Rushmore went in and found seats in the fourth row. On a platform ahead of them, the auctioneer was saying, "I have a hundred. Do I hear a hundred and ten?"

There was silence, then he continued, "I think you people don't realize the value of this beautiful cameo. It's worth much, much more. Come now, who'll give me a hundred and ten?"

"Mother, is it yours?" Honey whispered loudly.

"I can't tell," Mrs. Rushmore replied. "It's too far away for me to recognize." Her throat felt dry, and her voice was hoarse with tension.

The next instant Nancy called out, "One hundred and ten. And may we see the cameo? We came in late."

The auctioneer looked at the group and held the pin up. Then he said haughtily, "I'm sorry, but the viewing is over. We must get on with this. Ladies and gentlemen, I have a hundred and ten bid. Do I hear a hundred and fifteen?"

Mrs. Rushmore was beside herself. "Ladies, keep on bidding! We must get that cameo. It looks just like mine!"

"I have a hundred and ten bid," the auctioneer repeated. "Do I hear a bid for one hundred and fifteen?"

A man across the room called out, "One hundred and fifteen!"

The girls groaned. How much higher would they have to go?

The auctioneer said, "A hundred and fifteen. Do I hear a hundred and twenty?"

"A hundred and twenty!" Peg called out.

In his singsong voice the auctioneer continued to push up the price five dollars at a time. Whenever Nancy's group thought they had the bid, the man across the room would put in a higher bid.

Finally, the man bid a hundred and forty-five dollars. Once more the auctioneer pleaded with the audience.

"This exquisite cameo—why, it's a crime to even think of paying that small amount for what it's worth. Come now, who will give me a hundred and fifty dollars?"

Nancy offered to pay that much, and everyone waited for her opponent to go higher. But no matter how much the auctioneer pleaded, the man apparently had reached his limit.

"One hundred and fifty," the auctioneer said. "One hundred and fifty. Going—going—gone! Sold to the young lady who bid one hundred and fifty dollars. Please come forward with the money and take this beautiful cameo!"

Nancy looked at Mrs. Rushmore, who was rummaging in her purse. Then the woman went ashen white. "I don't have that much cash, and I forgot my checkbook. Girls, how much do you all have with you?"

Everyone counted, but together it came to no more than a hundred and twenty dollars.

"Step up, please," the auctioneer urged. "We must get on to the next item!"

As he turned to pick up a large package Nancy rushed toward the platform. Mrs. Rushmore and the girls stared in surprise. What was she going to do?

Fortunately, Nancy had tucked a couple of blank checks into her wallet. Now she walked to the desk where the purchased items were given out.

"Will you take my check?" she asked the man in charge.

"Yes, as long as you have identification. Your driver's license will be required."

Nancy nodded and wrote out the check. Then she handed it to the man along with her license. He copied the number and her address on the check, then gave the license back to her.

"And here's the pin," he added, handing her a small box. "Good luck!"

Nancy hurried back to her seat, hoping the cameo was the one Mrs. Rushmore had lost. The woman opened the package with shaking fingers.

"It's mine!" she murmured. "It's the queen's cameo! Oh, Nancy, how can I ever thank you for solving this mystery?"

Before Nancy could reply, Martie spoke up. "I'm very happy you got your property back. But I think it's a shame you had to buy it!"

"And I'll have to reimburse the insurance company," Mrs. Rushmore added.

Nancy leaned over and took the woman's ice-cold hand into her own. "Perhaps you didn't know this," she said, "but the sign up there says that all money taken in at the auction will be put into the special fund for widows and orphans of railroad men who have lost their lives in the line of duty. Why don't you just call the hundred and fifty dollars a donation to that worthy charity?"

Mrs. Rushmore's tearstained eyes looked into Nancy's. "Oh, you're wonderful, my dear. I'll do that."

## ACTIVITY

Nancy suggests that readers look in local newspapers under the Lost and Found columns and see if they can find any mysteries to solve.

# Chapter VIII

# The Mysterious
# Fortune-Teller
## *Palm Prints*

"GOOD morning, Mr. Drew," called out the members of the Detective Club. Sue added, "This is wonderful, having you speak to us."

Martie said, "And Nancy told us you'll give us a real case to solve."

Nancy's tall, handsome father smiled as he stood at one end of the living room facing the circle of girls before him. "Yes. I understand you have progressed so well in your detective work, I'll give you a real challenge. Are you ready?"

"Oh, yes!" the girls replied.

"The Rest-a-While Motel here in River Heights asked me to do some legal work for them, but there's also another problem you ladies could take care of."

Martie put up her hand. "Mr. Drew, isn't the Rest-a-While that motel up the river a ways?"

The lawyer nodded. "It has been open less than a year and is in a rather secluded spot. This is probably why certain guests like to stay there. The manager, Mr. Schwinn, suspects that a couple who registered as Mr. and Mrs. Tonio are fortune-tellers."

"How exciting!" Peg exclaimed.

"It's also against the law in River Heights," Mr. Drew pointed out.

Nancy asked, "Dad, why is Mr. Schwinn suspicious of these people?"

Her father said that a number of callers had gone to the couple's room. "There were strange people coming in and out at all hours of the day and night. Mr. Schwinn suspects that Mrs. Tonio charges them for telling their fortunes and has a thriving business going on in his motel."

"Would strange characters be going there just to have their fortunes told?" Sue asked.

The lawyer smiled. "That's what I want you to find out, if you can. I have no other information at this time. Now it's up to you. Let me know each day what you learn." He said good-bye and left the group.

Nancy took her father's place. The blackboard she had used so often was brought in, and the girls noticed that on it was the sketch of the palm of a human hand. Various sections had been marked with letters of the alphabet, and below was an explanation of what each one meant.

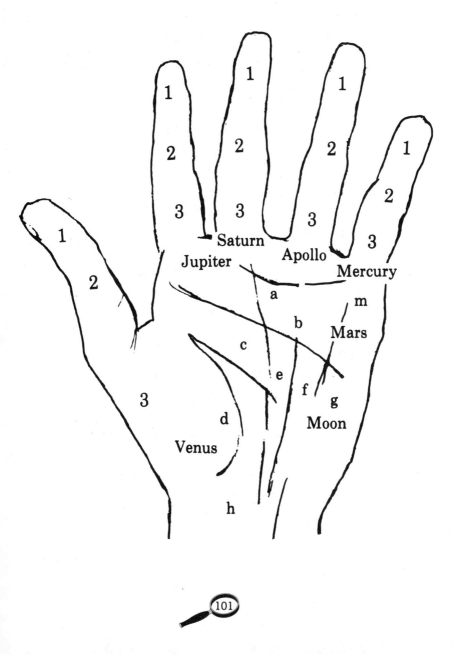

"Girls," said Nancy, "please get out your note-books and make a drawing of your own palms on one of the pages. Then copy the lines and letters from the blackboard."

As soon as her friends had finished making out-lines of their hands, Nancy explained:

"The fleshy humps on the lower end of each fin-ger and the side of the hand from the little finger to the wrist are mounts. You'll notice lots of wrinkles in your palm. These are called lines. The lines and mounts are supposed to tell about your character and the kind of life you have lived. Also, according to fortune-tellers, they show what will happen to you in the future."

Honey spoke up. "Do these mounts have names?"

"Yes," Nancy replied. "They're named after the planets. The one under the thumb is known as Ve-nus. Below the index finger is Jupiter, under the middle finger Saturn, then Apollo and Mercury. On the outer edge of the palm under Mercury is Mars, and below it is the Moon."

Cathy giggled. "Seems we have the whole uni-verse in our hands!"

Nancy grinned. "Now, let's look at the lines. The most important ones are indicated on this drawing. I hope you will memorize all these things because you never know when it will come in handy to know them—perhaps even tomorrow!"

## Mounts of the Hand

Venus—Charity, love, beauty.

Jupiter—Religiosity, ambition, love of honor, pride. On the negative side—arrogance, pompousness.

Saturn—Success, celebrity, intelligence, audacity. Small indicates meanness or love of obscurity.

Apollo—Wisdom, good fortune, prudence. When deficient—ignorance and failure.

Mercury—Love of knowledge, industry, aptitude for commerce, and in extreme forms, either love of gain and dishonesty or slackness and laziness.

Mars—Courage, resolution, rashness. Small indicates timidity.

Moon—Sensitiveness, morality, good conduct, imaginativeness. On the negative side— immorality, overbearing temper, and self-will.

## Lines and Parts

a. Ring of Venus: Sensitivity, could be directed either toward artistic experience or physical pleasure.

b. Line of Heart: Emotional and physical condition of heart.

c. Line of Head: Brainpower and state of mental health.

103

d. Line of Life: Vitality and length of life.

e. Line of Fate: Emotional and financial security, not visible in most hands.

f. Line of Fortune: Signs of talent and luck.

g. Line of Health: Digestion and physical health.

h. Bracelets: Ancient Greeks believed that the lines around the wrist could predict a woman's ease in childbearing. Some believe that each bracelet indictates twenty years of life expectancy.

"You must be kidding!" Peg protested. "I can't even remember simple things, like what day it is!"

The girls laughed, then Nancy went on. "I've marked the various lines with letters. Below the palm is the explanation."

Martie spoke up. "Haven't I heard that if a person has a high mount of Jupiter, he or she has a lot of pride and ambition?"

"That's right," Nancy replied. "Apollo denotes art and riches. Saturn stands for fatality, while Mercury indicates science and wit."

"I'll bet Venus stands for love," Karen said.

"That's correct. Also for music. And Mars shows cruelty and courage."

The girls studied their palms. Karen said excitedly, "I have a long life line!"

"Oh, dear," Peg exclaimed. "Mine is short."

"I wouldn't worry about it," Nancy told her. "Modern science has little use for palmistry."

"Are you expecting us to use this knowledge in finding out about the strange couple in the motel?"

"Perhaps," the young sleuth answered. "That's why I'd like you to learn whatever you can about palmistry. Then we'll plan our next move."

The girls studied the subject until lunchtime. Then while they were eating, Peg and Sue were given the assignment to ask the manager what had made him suspicious of the Tonios. Karen and Martie would talk to the chambermaid who took care of the Tonios' room, to see if she could come up with any clues. Cathy and Honey were to interview the waitress who served the Tonios' table, as well as any of the men who handled their baggage.

"I'll try to talk to the couple personally," Nancy said. "Wish me luck."

The meeting broke up, and the girls arranged to assemble later and report their findings.

As they filed out of the Drew living room, Sue remarked, "I hope that couple won't skip town before we have a chance to investigate them. After all our preparation, it would be such a disappointment!"

The next morning the club members arrived at Nancy's home again. All were eager to tell what they had learned at the motel.

Sue and Peg said they had had a hard time getting Mr. Schwinn to talk. "It wasn't until we told him that we were working for Mr. Drew," Peg explained, "that he would even speak to us. Then he telephoned your father, Nancy, who confirmed that it was all right to discuss the case with us."

Nancy remarked, "I can't blame him for being careful." She grinned at her students. "You could have been part of some gang!"

Sue and Peg burst into laughter.

"Tell us what Mr. Schwinn said," Martie begged.

Peg related that when the Tonios arrived, they had insisted upon carrying their own bags to room 315. "They were quite large. Mr. Schwinn was concerned that Mrs. Tonio was too small and delicate to be doing such heavy work."

Sue took up the story. "The next thing Mr. Tonio insisted upon was a private telephone line. Mr. Schwinn told us this was very unusual. Usually only VIPs get their own telephone line. However, it seems they got in touch with some friends, and the telephone was installed."

*"Hmm,"* said Nancy. "That's very interesting. The couple has connections with people of influence."

"Looks that way," Sue confirmed.

Since the two girls had nothing more to report, Karen and Martie told what they had found out at the Rest-a-While Motel.

"The chambermaid who takes care of the Tonios' room had a rather funny experience," Martie began. "The whole time she was cleaning up and tidying the room, the Tonios did not say a word, but kept staring at her. The girl felt very uncomfortable, and she guessed that the Tonios did not speak English. But according to Mr. Schwinn, they do!"

"And another thing," Karen added, "the chambermaid noticed a palmistry book on the table. When she picked it up, Mrs. Tonio grabbed the book immediately, as if she didn't want the girl to look inside."

"Strange," Nancy remarked. "Did anything else happen while she was in the Tonios' room?"

Martie replied, "The phone rang. Mrs. Tonio picked it up and scribbled notes on a pad, but she said nothing in reply. Then she hung up the receiver."

"It sounds weird," Peg remarked. "If I had been that chambermaid, I would have had chills going down my spine."

The other girls agreed that it was strange indeed and that this made the couple even more mysterious than before.

Now Cathy and Honey told their story. The waitress who served the Tonios' table had noticed that the couple never talked except to find fault with the food. They kept asking for all sorts of ethnic dishes that were not on the menu and fussed a great deal because they could not be made especially for them.

"What about you, Nancy?" Cathy asked. "Did you have any luck?"

"Yes and no," Nancy replied. "When I knocked on the Tonios' door, there was no answer. I knocked again, but still no one came to open it. So I walked up the hall, still wondering whether someone was in the room. Then I met the porter. On a chance, I asked him if he knew whether or not the Tonios were there."

"What did he say?" Peg asked eagerly.

"He said he thought so and wanted to know if I had knocked. When I said there had been no response, he said, 'I don't know if there's anything to it, but the other day I happened to be turning a corner and overheard someone mention the word *gypsy*. Then a woman went into the Tonios' room. Maybe she used it as a password.'"

"Did you try it, Nancy?" Karen inquired.

"Yes, but there still was no answer. The couple definitely must have been out."

Nancy said she expected her father any minute, and the girls should stay to tell him their findings. The lawyer arrived a short while later and listened with interest.

"You ladies have found out a great deal about the Tonios," he said. "I'll pass this information on to the FBI and the police to see if the couple are wanted for any criminal action. For the time being, continue with your work, and let me know if you learn anything else."

The Detective Club members discussed their next move. Nancy felt she should return to the motel and try to talk to the Tonios.

"Suppose you girls come along and, with the same partners, take positions in strategic spots. If the Tonios find out what we're up to and decide to get away, you'll be able to stop them. Cover the exits on their floor and the first floor."

The others agreed, and decided to meet at nine o'clock the following morning at the Rest-a-While Motel.

In the meantime, Nancy tried to figure out how she might trap the suspects. After a great deal of thought, she tucked a small can of talcum powder and a black cotton handkerchief into her handbag. She looked at her palm and whispered certain words over and over again, pointing to different areas on her hand.

"I guess I have it memorized all right," she finally told herself. "Oh, I hope it works!"

The club members were prompt, and Nancy and her friends set off by nine o'clock. They arrived at the motel half an hour later. All the girls except Nancy scattered in pairs to guard the various entrances.

Nancy walked into the motel and spoke to Mr. Schwinn. "I'm going to call on the Tonios again," she said. "Will you be here for the next hour or so? I might need your help."

"Yes. What's on your mind?"

Nancy said that she had high hopes of trapping the couple into revealing who they were and what they were doing in the motel. "I'm sure they're traveling under assumed names, but I'm trying a little trick to make them give away their identity."

Mr. Schwinn smiled. "I wish you luck. And I'll be ready."

Nancy went to room 315. No one was in the hallway when she knocked softly. She waited to give the couple enough time to come to the door, then she whispered through the crack, "Gypsy!"

There was a slight rustle inside. The young sleuth knocked again and said, "Gypsy, gypsy!"

Mr. Tonio opened the door. Nancy smiled and walked in. "Good morning," she said brightly. "Isn't it a beautiful day?"

Mr. Tonio looked a bit surprised, but did not ask her to leave. Nancy's heart was beating faster. Now she had jumped the first hurdle! Just then Mrs. Tonio appeared, dressed as a gypsy. "If you came to have your fortune told, you have wasted your time. I do not tell fortunes anymore," she said.

"Oh, I didn't come because of that," Nancy replied. "I have a message for you."

"What is it?" Mrs. Tonio seemed to become tense.

Nancy put a finger to her lips and motioned for the woman to sit down at a table. Then she pulled up a chair for herself, opened her handbag, and took out the black cotton handkerchief and the can of talcum powder.

While Mrs. Tonio stared at her in puzzlement, the young detective took the woman's right hand in her own and sprinkled her entire palm with the powder. Then she lifted Mrs. Tonio's arm and put her palm onto the black handkerchief, pressing down hard.

Mr. Tonio, who had been looking on in stunned silence, spoke up. "What are you doing?"

"Wait!" Nancy said softly.

She lifted Mrs. Tonio's hand from the handkerchief. On the cloth was a perfect palm print! Nancy was happy that the humps and lines showed perfectly. She pointed to the woman's lifeline and whispered, "In danger! Meet others at—" She stopped and pointed to the health line. Then she finished the sentence with the word *club*.

To be sure both Mr. and Mrs. Tonio had grasped the meaning of what she was trying to say, she went through the whole procedure again. The message was: *Your life is in danger. Meet others at health club.*

To Nancy's delight the couple looked at each other in surprise. Then both nodded. A wave of relief swept over the girl. Her ruse had worked! She picked up the handkerchief and powder, put them into her handbag, and left the room with a short nod, closing the door quietly behind her.

She hurried to Mr. Schwinn's office. The manager leaned over the counter eagerly.

"What happened?" he asked.

"I did it! At least I think I did!" Nancy replied. "The Tonios will be leaving and hopefully will lead us to their coconspirators. Please call the police and a man from the FBI to come here at once!"

Mr. Schwinn asked the girl to come into his private office and sit down while he made the calls. Within minutes four police officers arrived, and

"In danger! Meet others at club," Nancy whispered,
pointing to the woman's palm.

soon afterward, the FBI man appeared and introduced himself. They crowded into Mr. Schwinn's office.

"What's this all about?" the federal agent asked.

Before Nancy could answer, Mr. Schwinn put his finger to his lips and went to the counter, closing the door behind him. Mr. Tonio had walked up and wanted to pay his bill. The manager pulled a sheet from his file and took his guest's money, signing a receipt.

"Are you leaving now?" he asked.

"Yes. Will you please call a taxi for us?"

"Certainly. Would you like a bellman sent to your room?"

"No, no. That will not be necessary," Mr. Tonio replied, and hurried away. Mr. Schwinn went back into the office and informed everyone of Mr. Tonio's planned departure.

Nancy, meanwhile, had begun to tell the FBI agent and the police exactly what had happened, and described the couple.

"You say you took a palm print?" the FBI man asked. "May I see it?"

Nancy reached into her bag and pulled out the cotton handkerchief. The powder was slightly smudged, but most of the impression was clear enough.

After staring at it for a few moments, the man exclaimed, "See that scar through the mount of Jupiter? Without question this print was made by a woman not only the FBI but Interpol has been trying to find. She and her husband are wanted for a number of criminal activities both in Sicily and in various states of the U.S."

"Then they're not really fortune-tellers?" Nancy asked.

"Of course not. Their name is Vallecci, and they're known criminals."

Just then the couple came to the lobby, lugging their heavy bags. As they started for the front door, the FBI man and the four officers surrounded them, followed by Nancy and Mr. Schwinn.

"What does this mean?" Mr. Tonio demanded to know.

"It means you're under arrest," one of the officers replied. "We've been looking for you for a long time, Mr. and Mrs. Vallecci!"

The couple looked stunned, and the woman dropped her bag, staring in all directions fearfully. When she spied Nancy, an evil expression came into her eyes. "You—you are a spy! A wicked girl. You tricked us to set us up for the police!"

"Yes, I did," Nancy said. "My friends and I are detectives."

The other girls had arrived in the lobby and were crowding around the prisoners.

Mr. Tonio's face was a mask of anger. He hissed at his wife, "I told you, you would get us into trouble with your stupid fortune-telling!"

"Your own fortune won't be very fortunate," the FBI man said. "Come on now, let's get down to headquarters!"

With no route of escape open to them, the Valleccis followed the officers silently to the police car.

Mr. Schwinn wrung Nancy's hand. "You are amazing! Is there anything I can do for you?"

"I'd like to call my father and tell him the good news."

Mr. Drew was astounded that the case had been solved so quickly. "My special congratulations to you," he said. "Nancy, you caught a couple of really big fish!"

Nancy laughed. "One for you, Dad, and the other for the Detective Club!"

## ACTIVITY

Nancy suggests that you try to find your different palmistry lines and mounts and label your own personality traits and characteristics. Are they accurate? Compare your results with your friends'. Also, read their palms and see if you get the same results. Remember, this is all in good fun!

# CHAPTER IX

# THE DISAPPEARING FENCE
## *Testimony*

"TODAY," said Nancy to her club of aspiring detectives, "we have the privilege of attending a private hearing."

"How exciting!" Sue exclaimed. "Where will it be?"

"In my father's office," Nancy replied.

The club members begged her to tell them more about it. She said that the case concerned two neighbors who lived on farms outside River Heights.

"They've been squabbling over something that neither my father, who represents one of the men, nor the lawyer working for the other man thinks is worth taking to court. They'll try to settle the problem right in my dad's office."

Karen remarked, "This sounds like fun. What are we supposed to do?"

"Just listen," Nancy said. "We're to be like a jury."

She explained that a Mr. James was her father's client. The name of his neighbor was Jones. Both men had inherited the properties that had been in their families for years. The two small farms were separated by a narrow brook.

"Mr. James has a dog. Mr. Jones has a flower garden planted alongside the brook, and he sells the flowers to a florist," she went on. "In order to keep the dog from trampling his flowers, Mr. Jones put up a wire fence on the far side of the brook. Mr. James claims that it had been erected on his property, and therefore, he promptly took it down. Mr. Jones set it up again, saying it was on his property, and threatened to have the dog put down if Mr. James didn't keep him from splashing through the water and trampling the flower garden."

Nancy smiled. "Unfortunately, the dog didn't understand what it was all about and kept walking through the flowers. Mr. James insisted that when Mr. Jones had put the fence up, he had kept Mr. James from using the water for his farmwork. He also said that according to an old map he had found, his land went beyond the brook, and therefore, the flower garden actually belonged to him. He came to my father to see what could be done."

When the girls arrived at Mr. Drew's office, they found that one side of it had chairs assigned to them along the far wall. They took their seats, and in a few moments Mr. Drew walked in with two men. He introduced them to the girls as Mr. Bromley, an attorney, and Mr. Hallock, a retired judge.

Nancy's father explained that he had set up his office like a courtroom. Each attorney would interrogate James and Jones, then Mr. Hallock would render an opinion.

The judge took his position behind Mr. Drew's desk. The two lawyers sat on opposite ends of a bench, and a chair was placed near the judge.

Nancy's father walked over to the girls and said, "Be very attentive to details. Watch for any discrepancies in what Mr. James and Mr. Jones say. Plus, watch their facial expressions. Perhaps you can detect whether or not they're telling the truth and also notice any important evidence that is not brought forth. It may be a good idea to take notes."

The club members pulled out notepads from their handbags and announced that they were ready. Mr. Drew went into his assistant's office, where the two neighbors were waiting. First he asked Mr. James to come in, and directed him to the chair near the judge. Nancy whispered to the girls that it was a good idea to question each witness out of earshot of the other.

"Now, Mr. James, please tell us in your own words exactly what happened," Mr. Drew said to his client.

Mr. James stated that he was sure the property on which Mr. Jones had planted the flower garden belonged to him. "The flowers were pretty, and my family and I enjoyed them when we took a walk up to the brook," he said, "so we did not object. The trouble started when our dog, Prince, began to visit another dog and made his way through the brook and the flower garden to get there. We tried to teach him to go along the road instead, but had no luck. I followed him once to see how much damage he did to the flowers. He seemed very clever and walked around the roses without knocking anything down. But I admit he did leave paw prints."

Mr. Drew asked, "Are you saying that your dog did no damage to the garden?"

"Yes. He didn't trample the flowers as Mr. Jones claims. Besides, for the past two weeks we've kept him tied and walked with him on a leash."

"Now, how about the fence?" Mr. Drew went on. "Tell us about that."

Mr. James said that his neighbor had erected a wire fence without saying anything. "I became angry at this and told him he had put it on my property. That night, I took it down and threw it in his field. The following day, while my family was away, he put it up again."

Mr. Drew turned to Mr. Bromley and said, "Your witness."

The opposing lawyer began: "Mr. James, you say your dog never ruined the flowers? My client insists that they were trampled so badly that he had to replace them. Isn't it possible that you are not aware of the damage because new ones were planted?"

"He could not possibly have replanted them that quickly. I use that brook and see the flower bed every morning and every night."

Mr. Bromley smiled. "You have testified that your dog picked his way carefully among the plants and did not step on any of them. This is hard to believe. I have often seen dogs whip through flower beds, and it certainly didn't do the plants any good!"

The opposing lawyer turned to Mr. Drew. "I have no more questions."

Mr. James was excused and followed Mr. Drew from the office. Nancy's father now summoned Mr. Jones, who was shown to the seat near the judge.

Mr. Bromley questioned his client first. He asked him to name specific days when the dog had trampled the garden.

"Let me see," Mr. Jones said. "He was there last Tuesday or Wednesday. Then he damaged the rest of the plants on Friday night."

"How long has this problem been going on?" Mr. Bromley asked.

"We've argued about the dog crossing my land for years," Mr. Jones replied. "But it wasn't until I purchased special expensive plants that the real trouble began. Besides, the Jameses used to keep their dog in the house most of the time. But lately, they just let him roam a lot."

Mr. Bromley nodded and said, "Mr. Drew, your witness."

Nancy's father stood up. "What proof do you have, Mr. Jones, that the land in dispute is yours?"

"I have an old map. It shows that the brook belongs to me. I let Mr. James use the water until his dog became a nuisance."

Mr. James was brought in, and as his neighbor stepped down, he took the witness chair.

Mr. Drew repeated the various statements Mr. Jones had made. One by one, Mr. James refuted them. He and his family never let their dog out at night without having him on a leash. The problem over his roaming across the neighbor's land had never come up until the time Mr. Jones had plowed the area for his flower bed. He had declared that it belonged to him, and Mr. James had done nothing until the fence went up because he and his family enjoyed the beautiful flowers.

After a few more questions, the two men were shown into the assistant's office, while the attorneys and the judge discussed the matter.

All this time, Nancy and the Detective Club members had kept quiet and taken notes. Now they whispered in low tones, and all agreed that there were many discrepancies in the neighbors' testimony.

Mr. Hallock pointed this out also and said, "Gentlemen, you asked me to give my opinion in this case. I believe that both men are at fault in a way, and they should settle their differences on friendly terms. Would you like me to tell them this?"

Mr. Drew nodded and went to get the two neighbors, who came in arguing. Mr. Hallock rapped his knuckles on the desk and said, "Gentlemen, the three of us agree that both of you are at fault. We think you should forget your differences and get along on better terms. Mr. Jones, suppose you take down the offensive fence, and Mr. James, will you please keep your dog tied up or on a leash?"

There was silence for a couple of minutes, then Mr. Jones burst out, "I won't do it! I planted that garden. It belongs to me, and I don't trust that dog!"

Mr. James in turn said, "You can see why Mr. Jones and I don't get along. He doesn't trust me, and he makes up false stories to get his point across."

It was evident that neither man was going to give in. Mr. Drew and Mr. Bromley looked at each other. Nancy wondered if they were thinking, "Will it be necessary for this to be tried in court?"

Suddenly, Mr. Drew whispered to the judge and Mr. Bromley. The former nodded, and the opposing lawyer said after a moment, "Okay, go ahead."

Mr. Drew turned to the members of the Detective Club. "We've agreed that you ladies should give your opinion and suggest a possible procedure in this case."

Nancy was delighted and flattered by the suggestion. She looked at the girls, then at the lawyers, and said, "We have been comparing notes and find that the men's testimony is unconvincing. We recommend that each be asked to bring in the deeds to their property and whatever maps they may have, to determine the property line and who owns the flower garden."

"That's a very sensible solution," the judge agreed. "Mr. Drew, Mr. Bromley, I second the motion."

Mr. Jones burst out, "I won't do it!"

Mr. Drew did not seem surprised, but Mr. Bromley looked at the girls in awe. "Congratulations," he said. "You have figured out exactly what should be done."

Mr. James and Mr. Jones looked at Nancy and the club members. Finally both men declared they would have to go on a real hunt for the maps because unfortunately they had neglected to put them in bank safe-deposit boxes. They had been hidden in some desk or bureau drawer.

The next meeting of the group was set for several days later when, hopefully, the matter of the property line would be settled. The girls were eager for the time to arrive. Mr. Drew told Nancy that both men had accepted the old surveys made years before, which were used to write up the deeds and to make the maps.

"It's unfortunate they didn't have new ones made," Mr. Drew remarked. "Those old deeds and maps are hard to read. They're not computed in feet or yards, but in links and chains."

"How does that work?" Nancy asked.

Her father replied, "A long time ago, the surveyor carried a sixty-six-foot chain consisting of a hundred links to measure distances. Each link was approximately seven and nine-tenths inches long. If a piece of property was sixty feet, it was approximately ninety links of the chain."

"It sounds complicated," Nancy remarked.

Nevertheless, she set to work studying up on the subject. First, she took a book from her father's library, then went to the public library to get a surveyor's book. By the time the group reassembled in Mr. Drew's office, she had a good working knowledge of how to read old deeds and maps.

Those belonging to Mr. James and Mr. Jones were discolored and brittle, so they were handled carefully. Mr. Drew spread them out on his office desk, and Nancy was permitted to study the maps. To her amazement she discovered that both of them had been drawn by the same surveyor. She pointed this out to the men, who had been busy comparing the deeds. They nodded and went back to studying their documents.

The neighbors and their attorneys began to argue about what certain things meant. Nancy paid no attention to what they were saying. Her eyes and fingers followed certain lines on Mr. James's map as she studied the barely discernible measurements. After making some notes on her pad, she traced the borders on Mr. Jones's map.

Suddenly, she exclaimed, "Dad! Do you realize that these lines for the disputed property are exactly the same on both maps? Do you suppose—?"

Her father and the other men scrutinized the lines she had indicated. Mr. Drew took a magnifying glass from the desk drawer and placed it over the measurements.

"The area in question is exactly opposite on the two maps!" he said. "Now let's refer to the deeds and see if there are any similarities."

After reading both documents carefully, he and Mr. Bromley agreed that the deeds were correct but that the surveyor who had drawn the maps had followed the directions in Mr. James's deed of the area in dispute. He had inadvertently put those on Mr. Jones's map exactly in reverse.

Nancy whispered to her father, "Does this prove that the land belongs to Mr. James?"

"Without a doubt," he replied, and pointed this out to Mr. Bromley.

Before the opposing lawyer could answer, Mr. Jones cried out, "This isn't fair! Somewhere, at some time, someone pulled a bad error on my family!"

Mr. Drew remarked it was unfortunate neither Mr. James nor Mr. Jones had had the land surveyed when they had inherited the farms so the mistakes would have been found years before.

"Does this mean I lose the case?" Mr. Jones asked.

"I'm afraid it does," Mr. Bromley said. "I'm sorry, Mr. Jones." Then he turned to Mr. Drew. "Congratulations! Your daughter really won this case for you!"

Although Nancy was happy for her father's client, she felt sorry for Mr. Jones, who murmured over and over, "Now I'll have to give up my business of selling flowers. I can't afford to plant a new bed."

Nancy walked over to the members of the Detective Club and, for a few moments, held a whispered conversation with them. Finally she said, "Good. I'll tell him."

She returned to the desk, where the men were still lingering, and smiled at Mr. Jones. "I'm sorry you have to give up your beautiful garden. My friends and I want to offer our services to make a new one for you. We'll do all the digging and transplanting."

Mr. Jones looked at her in amazement. "You really mean it?" he asked hopefully.

By now the other girls were crowding around the desk. "Yes, we mean it!" they all said.

"That's most generous of you," Mr. Jones said. "You have no idea how bad I felt having to give up that garden."

The expression on his face had changed from one of sadness to a happy one. "I'll put the fence just inside my real property line, and you can make the garden right next to it. In that way both families can still enjoy the flowers."

Mr. James spoke up. "I'll pay for new ones to replace any that don't survive, and take as much water as you need from the brook."

## ACTIVITY

Nancy suggests that you go to your local library and see how your town or city was originally laid out. Look at aerial maps and see how your town has grown and changed over the years. Compare how your town looked when it was established with how it looks today.

# CHAPTER X

# THE HAUNTED HOUSE
*Sleuthing for a Ghost*

THE minutes of the previous meeting had been read, and the Detective Club was ready for another mystery.

The members looked toward Nancy, who now addressed the circle of girls.

"How many of you would like to track down a ghost?" she began.

"A real one or somebody playing ghost?" asked Peg.

Nancy said that nobody knew. "There's an old estate ten miles outside River Heights. At present no one lives there, but realtors who have taken prospective buyers to the place are scared away from it by ghostly figures and weird noises. The police have searched the premises but found no one."

Karen spoke up. "That sounds like a ghost all right."

Nancy told her that after the police had looked around the place, the strange happenings occurred only at night. She explained, "If we're going to try solving the mystery, we must go there in the evening."

The club members looked at one another, not sure that they wanted to visit a haunted house in the dark. Then they remembered several things that Nancy had taught them.

A good detective never gives up. A good detective must have no fear, only caution. A good detective must look for the unusual. A casual glance is not likely to turn up any evidence.

"I'm game!" Martie called out.

The other girls said, "We are, too."

Sue asked Nancy to tell them more about the mystery. The young sleuth said that the owners of the estate, a Mr. and Mrs. Costello, were elderly and not well. They were living in a nursing home and had appointed their niece, Maria Costello, to be their guardian.

"It was Maria," Nancy explained, "who came to me and asked if I would try to solve the mystery because she wants to sell the estate. She has keys to the house, the barn, and the stable, as well as to closets inside the mansion."

Cathy spoke up. "Wouldn't it be sensible for us to make our first trip in the daytime, in order to become familiar with the place? We'll have to know the layout to find our way around in the dark."

Nancy agreed and suggested that they go to Maria's house for the keys. "I'll phone her and see if she's at home. Maybe she can tell us more about the old estate."

Nancy called and learned that Maria would be happy to see the members of the Detective Club.

"I'm sure that you and your club can solve this puzzling mystery," Maria told the young detective.

Twenty minutes later Nancy introduced her friends to the Costellos' niece, a beautiful, dark-eyed woman, who invited them into her cheerful living room. They sat down.

A cart had been wheeled in on which stood a china pot of steaming hot cocoa and cups and saucers. On a plate next to them lay a mound of homemade cookies.

As the girls ate the delicious snack, Maria told them that the ghost or ghosts at the mansion were sometimes seen in filmy white garments, floating in the air toward the road.

"One group of people who went there with the thought of buying the place heard the weird sounds of a violin being played, yet no one was around. Naturally, the sale was lost. Other people reported a loud moaning coming from the third floor."

Maria stopped. "Have you heard enough?" she asked with a smile.

"That's plenty for me!" Karen declared. "You made chills go up and down my spine."

The others laughed, but some admitted the same thing had happened to them. Then Sue said slyly, "Of course, Maria, we don't dare let on to Nancy that we have any fears."

Maria laughed softly. "I'll get the keys."

While she was gone, Nancy said to her friends, "I suggest that during your sleuthing on this case you use everything you have learned since you joined the Detective Club."

Maria returned and handed over a large ring of keys to Nancy. Then the girls stood up to leave.

"I wish you luck," Maria said. "The expenses for my aunt and uncle are very high, and we really need to sell the estate. By the way, we are trying to have the new owner buy everything in the house rather than have an auction. I'm sure you'll be interested in looking at the old treasures."

The girls were surprised that the furnishings were still in the mansion.

Peg remarked, "Isn't it risky to leave all those things in the house while no one's living there? Burglars could steal everything."

Maria replied, "I have a feeling the ghost takes care of that!"

After the girls said good-bye to Maria, they drove several miles until they came to a country road marked Sleepy Hollow Drive. It was full of potholes, and the club members were jounced so much that Karen advised everyone to be quiet so that they would not bite their tongues! About a mile from the main road they reached a high picket fence with barbed wire on top.

"I wonder if the fence is electrified," Martie remarked.

"I doubt it," said Nancy. "Maria told me the power has been turned off. We'll need strong flashlights tonight."

The girls finally came to the big gate, and Nancy stopped the car. Looking through the pickets, she decided not to drive in. The entranceway was completely overgrown, and she did not want weeds and grass to wind themselves around the car's axles.

The girls got out and walked to the gate. Nancy took the key ring from her purse and inserted the larger keys into the lock one by one until she found a fancy brass key that fit perfectly.

The detective swung open one half of the enormous double gate, and the girls trooped inside. Then Nancy locked it again. As they picked their way along the barely discernible curving driveway, they spotted evidence of the former beauty of the landscape. Here and there bushes were in bloom, and fine old trees spread their branches. In one area, flowers struggled up between the choking weeds.

The mansion, constructed of yellow brick and partially covered with ivy, was huge. The girls went up the front steps, and Nancy unlocked the big door. As she pulled it open, it squeaked loudly.

Inside, there was dead silence. The club members walked around the center hall, admiring the winding stairway leading to the second floor. Before going up, however, they investigated all the rooms on the ground level. Each one was beautifully furnished, but dust covered everything.

"Let's watch for any telltale footprints," Nancy advised. "After all, the *ghost* may have been in here."

"Perhaps it's here right now," Honey muttered apprehensively, staring at a closet door, but not quite daring to open it.

"We'll have to look everywhere," Nancy said, and turned the knob. But they found no ghost in any of the closets or rooms, and no clue of any kind turned up. When they came to a door next to the kitchen and opened it, the door squeaked tremendously. Breathless, the young detectives waited to see what lay beyond. It was nothing but an empty pantry!

Martie heaved a sigh of relief. "I almost expected a skeleton to be hanging in there!" she said.

The girls were intrigued by the kitchen, which was large and had a fireplace.

"I suppose," said Sue, "that in olden days they used to cook food in this fireplace."

"*Perhaps the ghost is here right now,*" Honey said.

"Like barbecued hot dogs," Karen quipped, and everyone laughed.

"Well, that's it for the first floor," Nancy declared. "Let's go upstairs."

The steps were heavily carpeted, but a couple of the treads squeaked. The Detective Club members scrutinized them inch by inch but found nothing suspicious.

As the girls reached the top and started down the hall Cathy exclaimed, "Look! A man's footprints!"

There was a circle of impressions faintly visible in the dust that had settled on the dark oak floorboards. All of the girls stared at them in amazement.

"This is positively weird," Sue said finally. "Where did the man come from, and where did he go?"

Nancy looked at the ceiling. "That's the only place. But I see no evidence of a break-in or any tampering with the panels. Do you?"

Her friends shook their heads.

"Where do we go next?" Honey asked a bit apprehensively.

"To the bedrooms," Nancy said resolutely.

The search went on in silence until Cathy spoke up. "We're certainly advertising our visit," she said, and pointed to the trail of footprints the girls had been leaving.

"Maybe we'll scare the ghost," Sue said.

"One thing I'm sure of," Nancy said. "The ghost is

no thief. There are beautiful art objects in the rooms and lovely paintings on the walls. A thief would have taken all of them."

"Which makes it even harder for us to solve the mystery," Martie added.

The third floor yielded no clues, so the girls went to the basement. Since the electricity was switched off, the stairs were almost in total darkness. One part of the cellar, however, had a large window. Rays of sunlight were filtering through and illuminated the opposite wall.

Honey pointed to a series of letters that were crudely painted on it. "Look!" she called out. "What does this mean?"

The girls studied the strange writing, which read:

PAZF XUHQ TQDQ UR KAG HMXGQ KAGD XURQ

"It must be a code," Cathy remarked. "I'll bet the ghost left it."

"Let's try to figure it out," Sue said eagerly.

Quickly the girls pulled notepads from their handbags and tried all the codes they knew, but nothing fit. They listed the alphabet forward and backward, interposing letters, but finally turned to Nancy in despair.

"We give up!" Sue said. "Do you have any suggestions?"

"Try this," Nancy said. "Write the alphabet from *A* to *Z* in a horizontal line. Then underneath start with the second part of the alphabet, writing *M* under *A*, *N* under *B* and so forth until you come to *Z* under *N*. Then write the first part, putting *A* under *O*, *B* under *P* until you finish with *L* under *Z*."

The girls worked busily, applying the code to the message on the wall. Finally, Honey deciphered it.

"It says *DONT LIVE HERE IF YOU VALUE YOUR LIFE!*" she cried out. "Oh, how dreadful!"

"What do you think it means?" Sue asked.

"It could be a sinister warning that no one is safe on the premises," Cathy surmised, "or it could indicate that there's something unhealthy about this place. By living here, a person might become ill or even die!"

"Maybe that's what happened to Mr. and Mrs. Costello," Martie added. "You remember Maria said that they were in a nursing home. Perhaps they are there to recuperate from a disease they picked up here."

"That's not a very cheerful thought," Honey remarked.

"But a possibility," Nancy said, defending the statement. "However, I'm more inclined to think the ghost is trying to keep people from buying this property and is using the warning message to scare away anyone who's interested in it."

As the girls went back to the first floor Nancy

said, "What kind of an individual do you think the ghost is?"

"From the footprints we saw earlier, I'd say the ghost is a man," said Honey.

"And a pretty smart one," Peg continued. "Maybe he has a sense of humor."

"He enjoys playing tricks on people," Martie added.

"Well, I don't want him playing any tricks on me!" Karen declared emphatically.

Nancy said that she had noticed a photo album in the library. "It just occurred to me that it may contain a clue. I'd like to look at it again."

The club members followed Nancy into the large, wood-paneled room. The album lay on a table, and Nancy opened the first page.

"Everybody in the pictures is mentioned by name!" Peg said in surprise. "Here are Julia and James Costello, and all their brothers and sisters."

"They must be the owners of the place," Martie said.

"How do you know?" Peg asked.

"Because on the outside of the album it says 'Property of Julia and James Costello.'"

The book contained names of cousins, aunts, uncles, nieces, and nephews. "Apparently Mr. and Mrs. Costello had no children," Nancy said.

"Here's a picture of Maria," Peg pointed out. "It must have been taken a long time ago. She looks much younger in it."

Nancy flipped to another page. They came to a series of horses, each with a name and the word *thoroughbred* underneath.

"They're beautiful!" Martie exclaimed.

As Nancy turned the next page she said, "Here's a photograph of one of the horses with its groom. The horse is called Big Beauty, and the groom is Ben Wells."

Honey said she thought one of the persons in the album might be the ghost. "Perhaps we should memorize them all!"

Her remark was met with great sighs.

"Maybe only a few," Nancy told her. "Did you notice the tiny *d* alongside some of the names? My guess is that it stands for *deceased.* If we eliminate those people, our list won't be so long."

"The same applies to the horses," Cathy added. She went back to the pages where the animals were shown. There was a small *d* alongside the name of each horse.

"But the groom, Ben Wells, is apparently still living," she pointed out. "We should ask Maria where he is, and we should talk to him."

When they finished looking at the album, Nancy suggested that they all go outdoors. "We also have the barn and the stable to investigate," she said.

The girls started with the huge barn, which still had hay in the loft. But there was nothing else in the building, so they went to the stables.

"What a beautiful place!" exclaimed Karen, who was fond of horses and rode frequently. There were stalls on two sides of a wide aisle. "During bad winter weather the horses were probably exercised by being walked up and down the aisle," she added.

To the girls' amazement the stalls had beautifully polished mahogany sides, and the floors were spotlessly clean except for a layer of dust. Each enclosure had a three-quarter high door, with a picture of a horse hanging on it. Karen admired the animals in the photographs.

"Oh, here's one that shows Big Beauty and Ben Wells," she exclaimed.

All the girls looked at the pictures, then inspected the whole place thoroughly. There was no clue to a ghost, but Peg found a trapdoor in the floor. There was no ring with which to pull it up, only a small opening.

"It looks like a keyhole," she remarked.

Nancy took out her ring of keys and tried one after another. None fit.

Since there was no way to raise the trapdoor, the club members decided to continue their search outside. They strolled around the grounds but saw nothing suspicious. Finally, Nancy suggested that they go back home and get ready to return that evening.

She locked the big entrance gate, then the girls climbed into the car. On the way home they planned their evening's strategy.

It was decided that Cathy and Peg would watch the second and third floors of the house. Sue and Karen would take the first floor and nearby grounds, while Nancy, Honey, and Martie would observe the barn and stable.

The sun was setting when Nancy went from house to house picking up the club members. Each girl carried a strong flashlight, a stout cane in case of an attack, and a whistle.

One whistle blow would mean "I have seen something." Followed by another blow, the message would come from Cathy and Peg. Followed by two blows, it would be from Sue and Karen, and if there was one long blast after the first short one, it would be from Nancy, Honey, and Martie.

The girls reached the old estate in time to make their way to the designated posts before it was too dark to see where they were going. For nearly an hour there was no disturbance of any kind, and the club members wondered if they had come on a wild-goose chase.

Suddenly, Cathy and Peg, who were huddled near the second-floor stairway, were startled by an agonizing cry from the third floor. They tiptoed upstairs in the darkness. Just as they reached the landing, the two girls heard the cry again.

Quickly they turned on their strong flashlights and saw a man disappear through a door at the end of the hall! He closed it softly behind him, and there was a faint click. The girls rushed toward the door, but when Peg tried to open it, she realized that the man had locked it from the inside!

"We'd better tell the others," Cathy urged.

Keeping their lights on, the girls ran downstairs to the first floor. Just then Karen and Sue blew their whistles.

"Did you see the man?" Peg asked.

"No," Karen replied. "But we heard weird violin music. We flashed our lights around but couldn't see anything. It was positively spooky!"

"Where was it coming from?" Cathy asked.

"The parlor."

The four rushed into the room but found nothing. Peg concluded that the sounds could have come from the fireplace, and shone her light up the chimney. But the chimney made a turn, and they could see nothing above.

Cathy and Peg now told about the man who had disappeared through a door at the end of the third-floor hallway.

"He must know a route of escape," Karen said. "Let's go down to the basement and see if there are stairs coming from the third floor. We might have missed them the first time."

They descended the kitchen stairway and flashed their lights around the basement but saw nothing until Karen beamed her light up the fireplace chimney.

"Girls, look!" she cried out. "There's a ladder fastened to one wall, and it goes all the way up! Obviously, this is where the man came down!"

Karen and the others continued their hunt through the cellar. When they reached the room where the code had been printed on the wall, they were startled to see that it had been underlined twice with red crayon!

"The ghost has been here!" Peg exclaimed. She and her friends looked at the markings with new interest. The upper crayoned line was straight, but at the right end of it, the line curved downward into two loops. The lower line looked like a picture of jagged lightning.

Sue asked, "Do you suppose there's a message in these lines?"

The girls studied them for a while, then Karen had an inspiration. "The loops at the end of the top line form a *B*. The lower line looks like a series of *W*s."

"Meaning," Sue cried out, "that this code could have been written by Ben Wells!"

While the four girls stared at the marks, Nancy, Honey, and Martie were having an adventure of their own. A mysterious light had suddenly appeared in the garden, showing a white figure swaying along the treetops and heading for the entrance gate. The three followed it excitedly, but after a few moments it disappeared.

*"This is where the man came down!"* Karen cried out.

Just then they heard a horse neigh in the stable. The girls rushed inside. There was no horse in sight!

"The ghost again!" Honey said.

Nancy dashed toward the trapdoor. It was wide open, and a man was descending into the darkness!

On a hunch Nancy cried out, "Stop, Ben Wells! We've found you! You can't play ghost any longer!"

The man was so amazed at being called by name that he stood still. The three girls ran up to him, but Honey paused long enough to blow her whistle sharply, followed by a long blast.

Karen, Peg, Sue, and Cathy heard the signal as they were coming out of the mansion. They practically flew toward the stable and gasped in surprise when they saw the trapped man.

"How did you know my name?" he asked.

Nancy replied, "We saw your picture in an album beside a horse named Big Beauty."

"And you're the ghost!" Peg exclaimed. "We figured out those two red crayoned lines you put under the code you wrote. The top one forms a *B*, and underneath is a series of *W*s. You're Ben Wells!"

"I didn't think anybody would ever find out," the groom said, hanging his head. He stepped up to the floor and closed the trapdoor. "I haven't done any harm here," he added. "Nobody can accuse me of that!"

"You certainly scared a lot of people!" Nancy said. "Why?"

"I've always loved this place. I worked here as a boy and later as a groom. Mr. and Mrs. Costello were very good to me, and I admit I was wrong in trying to prevent the place from being sold. But I wanted it for myself. So I played ghostly tricks to keep people away."

"How did you get in?" Sue questioned.

"I have duplicate keys to everything in the mansion," Wells replied. "Also to the barn and stable. When Mr. and Mrs. Costello became ill and had to go to the nursing home, I was dismissed. It broke my heart, and after a few days I decided to come back and live here by myself. But I was sure not to leave any food or clothes where people could find them."

Karen spoke up. "Didn't it ever occur to you that the new owners might have horses and would need a groom?"

Wells shrugged. "They might have their own. Why should they hire me?"

He explained that he knew about the secret ladder in the chimney and the various underground hideouts. "There's a series of tunnels beneath the mansion that lead to the different outbuildings. They're really old. The Costellos did not build them, but I found the tunnels and pointed them out to my employers. They said I should keep the secret because visitors might get hurt in them."

Honey asked, "How about the shoe prints on the second floor? They don't go anywhere!"

Ben grinned. "There's a hidden ladder in the second-floor ceiling. I climbed down, made a few prints, and went up again. You can't tell where the ladder is because of the design on the paneled ceiling."

Sue asked Ben Wells how he knew about codes and how he did his various tricks.

"My father was a magician," the man replied. "I learned a lot of things from him. Some of the gadgets I used while playing ghost I built myself; others I bought, like the violin tape."

He paused momentarily, then asked, "Did you figure out the code?"

"Yes, we did," the girls replied.

Ben Wells was not sure that they were telling the truth and asked them what it meant.

*"Don't live here if you value your life,"* Honey said.

Wells shook his head in amazement. "You ladies certainly are smart." He sighed. "What are you going to do to me?"

The club members waited for Nancy to speak. She said, "Come with us to my car."

If Ben had any idea of resisting, he knew it was hopeless with seven strong, healthy girls watching him. He meekly went along with them. Nancy unlocked the entrance gate, and they let themselves out. At the car she used her new cell phone and contacted Chief McGinnis at police headquarters.

Quickly she told him the Costello mystery had been solved. Would the chief please call her father and come to the estate with him at once? The officer promised to do so.

While they were waiting, Ben said cheerfully, "How would you like to see a few sleight-of-hand tricks?"

The girls told him they would, so Ben pulled several handkerchiefs from his pocket, knotted them, and rolled them in his hand. Presently, he plucked at the corner of one, and out came all the others, no longer tied together.

"That's great!" said Sue, and Ben did several other well-known tricks, like taking money out of Karen's ear and turning a light on Honey's shoes to make them appear to be green.

Finally the groom looked up at the girls. "I take it you're all amateur detectives. Would you like me to teach you some of the sleight-of-hand tricks? They may come in handy in your work."

Before the girls had a chance to answer, Chief McGinnis and Mr. Drew drove up. Everything was explained to them, and they decided to take Ben Wells back to headquarters for further questioning.

As the car pulled away, Ben leaned out a window. "Any time you want to learn some tricks, get in touch with me!" he called.

## ACTIVITY

Readers: Here's another code for you to try to crack.
The answer is on page 152.
Good luck!

E KSSH HIXIGXMZI QYWX PSSO
JSV XLI YRYWYEP E GEWYEP KPERGI MW
RSXPMOIPC XS XYVR YT ERC IZMHIRGI

## ANSWERS TO CODES

Answer to code on page 50: A good detective absolutely never gives up.

Answer to code on page 150: A good detective must look for the unusual. A casual glance is not likely to turn up any evidence.